Nature

Nature

Ferguson
An imprint of Infobase Publishing

Nature

Ferguson
An imprint of Infobase Publishing
132 West 31st Street
New York NY 10001

Library of Congress Cataloging-in-Publication Data

Nature.
   p. cm. — (Discovering careers)
 Includes bibliographical references and index.
 ISBN-13: 978-0-8160-8046-5 (hardcover : alk. paper)
 ISBN-10: 0-8160-8046-1 (hardcover : alk. paper) 1. Natural history—Vocational guidance—Juvenile literature. 2. Nature conservation—Vocational guidance—Juvenile literature. I. J.G. Ferguson Publishing Company. II. Title: Nature.
 QH49.N49 2010
 508.023—dc22
                   2009031906

Ferguson books are available at special discounts when purchased in bulk quantities for businesses, associations, institutions, or sales promotions. Please call our Special Sales Department in New York at (212) 967-8800 or (800) 322-8755.

You can find Ferguson on the World Wide Web at http://ferguson.infobase publishing.com

Text design by Erik Lindstrom and Erika K. Arroyo
Cover design by Takeshi Takahashi
Composition by Mary Susan Ryan-Flynn
Cover printed by Bang Printing, Brainerd, MN
Book printed and bound by Bang Printing, Brainerd, MN
Date printed: September 2010
Printed in the United States of America

10 9 8 7 6 5 4 3 2 1

CONTENTS

Introduction

You may not have decided yet what you want to be in the future. And you don't have to decide right away. You do know that right now you are interested in nature. Do any of the statements below describe you? If so, you may want to begin thinking about what a career in nature or the environment might mean for you.

_____ Science is my favorite subject in school.
_____ I am concerned about endangered species.
_____ I enjoy being outdoors.
_____ I am interested in wild animals.
_____ I like to study the plants and trees native to my area.
_____ I spend a lot of time hiking in the woods or through parks.
_____ I worry about air, water, and soil pollution.
_____ I participate in community cleanup projects.
_____ I would rather live in the country than in a city.
_____ My main hobby is gardening.
_____ It upsets me to hear about events like oil spills and rain forest destruction.
_____ I am interested in farming and agriculture.

Discovering Careers: Nature is a book about careers in nature, from biologists to zoologists. Nature careers involve working with wild animals, plants and trees, soil and land, and water. Some nature fields, such as biology, botany, geology, and zoology careers, focus on studying and learning more about the natural world. Others, such as ecology, pollution control, land preservation, and forestry careers, work at conserving and protecting the world. People in nature-related careers are interested in and deeply concerned about how humans interact with and change our planet.

This book describes many possibilities for future careers in nature. Read through it and see how the different careers are connected. For example, if you are interested in animal life, you will want to read the chapters on Biologists, Fish and Game Wardens, Naturalists, Oceanographers, Park Rangers, Wildlife Photographers, and Zoologists. If you are interested in ecology, you will want to read the chapters on Ecologists, Environmental Engineers, Foresters, Land Trust or Preserve Managers, and Soil Conservationists and Technicians, and Soil Scientists. Go ahead and explore!

What Do Nature Workers Do?

The first section of each chapter begins with a heading such as "What Botanists Do" or "What Range Managers Do." It tells what it's like to work at this job. It describes typical responsibilities and assignments. You will find out about working conditions. Which workers spend most of their time outdoors in fields and forests, on rangeland, or on a ship in the ocean? Which ones work in laboratories or offices? This section answers all these questions.

Education and Training

This section tells you what classes and education you need for employment in each job—a high school diploma, training at a junior college, a college degree, or more. It also talks about on-the-job training that you could expect to receive after you're hired and whether or not you must complete an apprenticeship program.

Earnings

This section gives the average salary figures for the job described in the chapter. These figures provide you with a general idea of how much money people with this job can make. Keep in mind that many people really earn more or less than the amounts given here because actual salaries depend on many different things, such as the size of the company, the location of the company, and the amount of education, training, and experience you have. Generally, but not always, bigger companies or organizations located in major cities pay more than smaller ones in smaller cities and towns, and people with more education, training, and experience earn more. Additionally, federal agencies—such as the Environmental Protection Agency—pay more than those at the state level. Also remember that these figures are current averages. They will probably be different by the time you are ready to enter the workforce.

Outlook

This section discusses the employment outlook for the career: whether the total number of people employed in this career will increase or decrease in the coming years and whether jobs in this field will be easy or hard to find. These predictions are based on economic conditions, the size and makeup of the population, foreign competition, and new technology.

Keep in mind that these predictions are general statements. No one knows for sure what the future will be like. Also remember that the employment outlook is a general statement about an industry and does not necessarily apply to everyone. A determined and talented person may be able to find a job in an industry or career with the worst kind of outlook. And a person without ambition and the proper training will find it difficult to find a job in even a booming industry or career field.

For More Info

Each chapter includes a sidebar called "For More Info." It lists organizations that you can contact to find out more about the field and careers in the field. You will find names, addresses, phone numbers, email addresses, and Web sites.

Extras

Every chapter has a few extras. There are photos that show workers in action. There are sidebars and notes on ways to explore the field, fun facts, profiles of people in the field, tips on important skills for success in the field, information on work settings, lists of Web sites and books, and other resources that might be helpful.

At the end of the book you will find three additional sections: "Glossary," "Browse and Learn More," and "Index." The Glossary gives brief definitions of words that relate to education, career training, or employment that you may be unfamiliar with. The Browse and Learn More section lists nature-related books, periodicals, and Web sites to explore. The Index includes all the job titles mentioned in the book.

It's not too soon to think about your future. We hope you discover several possible career choices. Happy hunting!

Adventure Travel Specialists

What Adventure Travel Specialists Do

Adventure travel specialists plan, and sometimes lead, tours of unusual, exotic, remote, or wilderness places. Most adventure travel involves some physical activity that takes place outdoors. There are two kinds of adventure travel—*hard* and *soft adventure.* Hard adventure involves high physical activity and advanced skill. Some examples of hard adventure are mountain biking, white-water rafting, or rock climbing. Soft adventure, such as hot air ballooning, horseback riding, or bird watching, is less physical and more family-oriented.

A popular type of adventure travel is the ecotour. This kind of trip combines the exciting thrill of adventure with travel to natural areas that conserve the environment and respect the well-being of the local people. A tour of the Asian rain forests, a trek to the Amazon jungle, or a trip to the Galapagos Islands are some examples of ecotours.

Some adventure travel specialists work in offices planning trips. They make transportation arrangements, order supplies, arrange lodging, and all other details for a successful vacation. They also promote and sell tour packages. Specialists that lead the tours are called *outfitters.* Some adventure specialists both plan and lead tours.

Outfitters and guides demonstrate any activities involved on the trip, help with the equipment, or assist any group member having difficulties. They also speak about the location, scenery, history, wildlife, and unusual aspects of the region where the group is traveling. Guides help tour members

EXPLORING

- Read magazines, such as *Outside* (http://www.outsidemag.com), *Backpacker* (http://www.backpacker.com), *National Geographic Adventure* (http://www.nationalgeographic.com/adventure), and *Bicycling* (http://www.bicycling.com).
- Research environmental groups, such as the National Audubon Society (http://www.audubon.org), National Wildlife Federation (http://www.nwf.org), and Sierra Club (http://www.sierraclub.org).
- Explore hobbies, such as scuba diving, sailing, hiking, mountain biking, canoeing, or fishing. Check your local phone directory for clubs and organizations that focus on these specialties.
- Another way to explore this field is to go on an adventure outing yourself. Outward Bound USA, for example, offers a wide variety of programs for teenagers, college students, and adults. And don't forget to check out summer camp options. YMCA camps, scouting camps, and others provide the opportunity to learn about the outdoors and improve your camping skills. Summer camps are also excellent places to gain hands-on experience as a worker, whether you are a counselor, a cook, or an activity instructor.

in emergency situations, or during unplanned events. They are prepared to handle injuries, dangerous areas, and crisis situations.

Education and Training

High school classes such as geography, social studies, and history will prepare you for work as an adventure travel specialist. Speech or English classes will improve your public speak-

Tips for Success

To be a successful adventure travel specialist, you should

- care about protecting the environment
- love the outdoors
- be physically fit

- be responsible
- have leadership abilities
- have good business skills
- be organized

ing skills. If you specialize in ecotravel, then study subjects such as earth science, biology, geology, and anthropology. A college degree is not required, but many companies prefer to

White-water rafting guides roar through rapids on the Yellowstone River near Gardiner, Montana. They travel the canyon during high water so they can better understand dangerous areas that may pose a risk to their clients. (Garrett Cheen, The Livingston Enterprise/AP Photo)

hire those who have earned one, especially a degree in health, physical education, or recreation. If you plan to manage your own travel business someday, you should take a class in business administration, either at a university or a trade school.

Your experience and skill in a physical activity is important in this career. Take classes or join clubs in your area of interest, such as rock climbing, ballooning, or photographing wildlife. Certain activities, such as scuba diving, may require formal training and a license examination. All travel guides should have training in emergency first aid and CPR.

Earnings

Factors that influence earnings for adventure travel specialists include experience, type of employer, and amount of work done. According to one university offering programs in adventure travel, graduates can make between $125 and $225

FOR MORE INFO

For industry information, contact
Adventure Travel Trade Association
601 Union Street, 42nd Floor
Seattle, WA 98101-2341
360-805-3131
http://www.adventuretravel.biz

For information on the ecotourism industry and related careers, contact
International Ecotourism Society
1333 H Street, NW, Suite 300, East Tower
Washington, DC 20005-4707

202-347-9203
info@ecotourism.org
http://www.ecotourism.org

Visit the association's Web site for the latest adventure travel news.
Outdoor Industry Association
4909 Pearl East Circle, Suite 200
Boulder, CO 80301-2499
303-444-3353
info@outdoorindustry.org
http://www.outdoorindustry.org

per day, or $17,000 for a three- to four-month season. Experienced guides with some managerial responsibilities can earn up to $65,000 a year. Tour leaders receive free food and accommodations, as well as a daily allowance while conducting a tour.

Many experienced adventure travel specialists start their own business and work for themselves. Those who own their own business who work year round earn anywhere from $25,000 to more than $150,000 annually.

Outlook

There is a growing demand for adventure travel. This is because more people are interested in the environment and conservation, as well as physical fitness. One-half all U.S. traveling adults, or about 98 million people, have taken an adventure trip in their lifetime, according to the *Adventure Travel Report*. This suggests that the field is popular and will continue to be so in the future. There is a lot of competition for adventure travel jobs. Hundreds of people may apply for a single job. Many adventure travel specialists have to work one or two other jobs just to have enough money to live. Those with experience in adventure travel or a unique specialty will have the best chances for employment.

Biologists

What Biologists Do

Biologists are scientists who study how plants and animals grow and reproduce. They are sometimes called *biological scientists* or *life scientists.* Biologists often have other job titles because they specialize in one area of biology. *Botanists,* for example, study different types of plants. *Wildlife biologists* study the habitats and the conditions necessary for the survival of birds and other wildlife. *Zoologists* study different types of animals. They are usually identified by the animals they study: *ichthyologists* (fish), *mammalogists* (mammals), *ornithologists* (birds), and *herpetologists* (reptiles and amphibians).

Biologists conduct research in the field or in the laboratory. Their exact job duties vary depending on their area of interest. For example, *aquatic biologists* study plants and animals that live in water. They may do much of their research on a boat. They study the water temperature, amount of light, salt levels, and other environmental conditions in the

EXPLORING

- You can learn about the work of biologists by taking school field trips to nature centers, laboratories, parks, research centers, aquariums, and zoos.
- Many park districts offer classes and field trips to help you explore plant and animal life. Take part in these activities to learn more about the field.
- Talk to a biologist about his or her career. Ask the following questions: What made you want to become a biologist? Where do you work? What do you like most and least about your job? How did you train to become a biologist? What advice would you give to someone who is interested in the career?

oceans, streams, rivers, or lakes. They then observe how fish and other plants and animals react to these environments. *Marine biologists* are specialized aquatic biologists who focus on plants and animals that live in oceans. *Entomologists* study insects and their relationship to other life forms. *Limnologists study* freshwater organisms and their environment. *Mycologists* study edible, poisonous, and parasitic fungi, such as mushrooms, molds, yeasts, and mildews, to determine which are useful to medicine, agriculture, and industry.

No matter what type of research biologists do, they must keep careful records to note all procedures and results. Because biologists may sometimes work with dangerous chemicals and other materials, they always must take safety precautions and carefully follow each step in an experiment.

Some biologists give advice to businesses and government agencies. Others inspect foods and other products. Many biologists write articles for scientific journals. Some may also teach at schools or universities.

Biologists need to be good at conducting research and solving problems. They should also have patience because they often spend much time in observation in laboratories and in the field. Biologists must also have good communication skills in order to work well with others and explain their findings orally and in writing.

DID YOU KNOW?

- There are approximately 1.8 million species of animals, plants, and other living things on earth.
- There are five kingdoms of life on earth: monera (single-celled organisms that do not have a nucleus, or a control center; bacteria are the only type of monera); protists (single-celled organisms that have a nucleus—examples include algae and amoeba); fungi (examples includes mushrooms and molds); plants; and animals.
- There are about 260,000 plant species on earth.

Education and Training

If you are thinking about a career in biology, you should plan to take high school courses in biology, chemistry, mathematics, physics, and a foreign language.

A biologist (right) and an assistant feed baby parrots that were rescued from animal traffickers. (Eraldo Peres, AP Images)

After high school, you must go to college, where you will take more advanced courses in biology, math, chemistry, and physics. Then you choose a specialty. Specialties include microbiology, bacteriology, botany, ecology, or anatomy. Most successful biologists also have a master's degree or a doctorate in biology or a related field.

Earnings

Salaries for biologists ranged from $36,000 to more than $98,000 a year in 2007, according to the U.S. Department of Labor. The average salary is $63,000. Government biologists with bachelor's

FOR MORE INFO

For information about a career as a biologist, contact
American Institute of Biological Sciences
1444 I Street, NW, Suite 200
Washington, DC 20005-6535
202-628-1500
http://www.aibs.org

For career information for middle and high school students, visit the society's Web site.
American Society for Microbiology
1752 N Street, NW
Washington, DC 20036-2904
202-737-3600
http://www.asm.org

degrees earned salaries of about $68,500 a year. Microbiologists earned median salaries of $60,000; zoologists and wildlife biologists, $55,000; and college biology professors, $71,000.

Outlook

Employment for biologists should be good in the future. Biologists will continue to be needed to help solve environmental problems. Botanists, zoologists, and marine biologists will have good employment prospects. Only a small number of people work in this field, so there will always be competition for good jobs.

Biologists who have advanced degrees will have the best chances of obtaining challenging and good-paying jobs. Those with only a bachelor's degree will find work as science or engineering technicians, health technologists and technicians, and high school biology teachers.

Botanists

What Botanists Do

Botanists are scientists who study plants. They study cell structure; how plants reproduce; how plants are distributed on earth; how rainfall, climate, and other conditions affect them; and more.

Botany is a major branch of biology. Botanists play an important part in modern science and industry. Their work affects agriculture, agronomy (soil and crop science), conservation, forestry, and horticulture. Botanists develop new drugs to treat diseases. They find more food resources for people in poor countries. They discover solutions to environmental problems.

EXPLORING

- Visit the following Web sites to view photos of plants: Steve's Plant Image Database (http://arnica.csustan.edu/photos/plants.asp), KidScienceLink.com (http://www.kidsciencelink.com/botany), and Botanical Society of America (http://www.botany.org/plantimages).

- Grow your own garden, including fruits and vegetables, herbs, flowers, and indoor plants. Keep a notebook to record how each plant responds to watering, fertilizing, and sunlight.

- Take camping trips or hike to learn more about the natural world.

Words to Learn

biomes a large community of organisms in a single area; examples of biomes are the tropical rain forest, the prairie, the tundra, and the desert

community A group of organisms that share a particular habitat

conservation The practice of preserving natural resources

ecosystem A group of organisms living together with nonliving components

global warming The slow rise in our planet's average temperature caused by an increase in greenhouse gases (such as carbon dioxide, methane, and nitrous oxide)

habitat An area where an organism or group of organisms normally lives

horticulture The cultivation of plants

inventory of species Counting the number of different types of plants or animals in a given area

Botanists who specialize in agriculture or agronomy try to develop new varieties of crops that better resist disease. Or they may try to improve the growth of crops such as high-yield corn. These botanists focus on a specific type of plant species, such as ferns (pteridology), or plants that are native to a specific area, such as wetland or desert. Some botanists work in private industry at food or drug companies. They may develop new products or they may test and inspect products.

Research botanists work at research stations at colleges and universities and botanical gardens. Botanists who work in conservation or ecology often do their work out in the field. They help recreate lost or damaged ecosystems, direct pollution cleanups, and take inventories of species.

There are many different types of botanists. *Ethnobotanists* study how plants are used by a particular culture or ethnic group to treat diseases and injuries. *Ecologists* study the connection between plants and animals and the physical environment. They restore native species to areas, repair damaged ecosystems, and work on pollution problems. *Forest ecologists* focus on forest species and their habitats, such as forest wetlands. *Mycologists* study fungi and apply their findings to medicine, agriculture, and industry. Mushrooms and yeast are examples of fungi. *Plant cytologists* use powerful microscopes to study plant tissues in order to discover why some cells become malignant (unhealthy) and cause the plant to get sick or die. *Plant geneticists* study the origin and development of inherited traits (or qualities), such as size and color.

Other botanical specialists include *morphologists*, who study macroscopic plant forms and life cycles (or those that can be viewed by the human eye); *palyologists*, who study pollen and spores; *pteridologists*, who study ferns and other related plants; *bryologists*, who study mosses and similar plants; and *lichenologists*, who study lichens, which are dual organisms made of both alga and fungus.

Botanists have a deep love for plants and nature, but also enjoy science. They should be very organized, have curious per-

DID YOU KNOW?

Where Botanists Work

- Federal agencies, including the Department of Agriculture, Environmental Protection Agency, Public Health Service, Biological Resources Discipline, and the National Aeronautics and Space Administration
- Local and state agencies
- Colleges and universities
- Greenhouses
- Arboretums
- Herbariums
- Seed and nursery companies
- Fruit growers
- Agribusiness, biotechnology, biological supply, chemical, environmental, food, lumber and paper, pharmaceutical, and petrochemical companies

FOR MORE INFO

Visit the society's Web site for information on careers in botany.

Botanical Society of America
PO Box 299
St. Louis, MO 63166-0299
314-577-9566
http://www.botany.org

Contact this organization for information on volunteer positions in natural resource management for high school students.

Student Conservation Association
689 River Road
PO Box 550
Charlestown, NH 03603-0550
603-543-1700
ask-us@thesca.org
http://www.thesca.org

sonalities, and be able to work well alone or with other people. They should also have good communication skills.

Education and Training

In high school, take as many biology and earth science classes as possible. You should also take college prep courses in chemistry, physics, mathematics, English, and foreign language.

If you want to become a botanist, you will have to go to college and earn a bachelor's degree. People who want to work in research and teaching positions have to study even longer. They go on to earn a master's or even a doctoral degree. These higher degrees require you to specialize in one of the many areas of botany mentioned in the section, What Botanists Do. For example, a master's in conservation biology focuses on the conservation of specific plant and animal communities.

Earnings

The National Association of Colleges and Employers reports that those with a bachelor's degree in biological and life sciences earned average starting salaries of $34,953 in 2007. Most botanists earned between $48,000 and $72,000 in 2009, according to Salary.com. The most experienced botanists earned more than $84,000 a year.

Outlook

Employment for botanists is expected to be good. Botanists will be needed to help with environmental, conservation, and pharmaceutical issues. Botanists work in such a wide variety of fields that they are almost guaranteed to have a job.

Employment for botanists who work for the government may not be as strong. When the economy is weak, government agencies may have less funding to hire botanists. When the economy is strong, there will be more money to hire botanists to conduct research.

Botanists with advanced degrees and years of experience in the field will have the best job prospects.

Ecologists

What Ecologists Do

Ecologists are specialized scientists. They study how plants and animals interact with and sustain each other in their environments, or habitat. An environment includes living things. It also includes nonliving elements, such as chemicals, moisture, soil, light, temperature, and things made by humans, such as buildings, highways, machines, fertilizers, and medicines. The word ecology is sometimes used to describe the balance of nature.

EXPLORING

- Read books and other publications about ecology and the environment. You will find lots of reading material at your library or bookstore and on the Internet.
- Join a school ecology club.
- Visit natural history museums to learn more about the field. Visit nearby parks or forest preserves. What kinds of trees and plants grow there?

Which insects, animals, and birds are native to the area?
- Talk to an ecologist about his or her career. Ask the following questions: What made you want to become an ecologist? What do you like most and least about your job? How did you train to become an ecologist? What advice would you give to someone who is interested in the career?

Tips for Success

To be a successful ecologist, you should

- love and respect nature
- know a lot about the environment
- be able to work well with others
- be a good problem solver
- have good communication skills
- be willing to work outside in all types of weather conditions

A big part of an ecologist's job is to study communities. A community is the group of organisms that share a particular habitat. For example, a *forest ecologist* might study how changes in the environment affect forests. They may study what causes a certain type of tree to grow well, including light and soil requirements, and resistance to insects and disease.

Some ecologists study biomes, which are large communities. Examples of biomes are the tropical rain forest, the prairie, the tundra, and the desert. The ocean is sometimes considered as one biome.

Many ecologists study ecosystems—a living community together with its nonliving components. *Population ecologists* study why a certain population of living things increases, decreases, or remains stable.

All living things, including humans, depend on their environments to live. As a result, the work of ecologists is extremely important in helping us understand how environments work. An example of how the study of ecology helps us is farming. Ecologists help farmers grow crops in the right soils and climates, provide livestock with suitable food and shelter, and get rid of harmful pests, such as insects or other animals that eat or damage crops. The study of ecology helps protect, improve, and preserve our environment. Ecologists study industry and government actions and help fix past environmental problems.

Most ecologists work in land and water conservation jobs in the public sector. This includes the federal government, the largest employer. The Bureau of Land Management, the U.S. Fish

A U.S. Forest Service ecologist marks a tree above the location of a trap he set to study amphibians in a pond. (Elaine Thompson, AP Images)

and Wildlife Service, the National Park Service, and the U.S. Geological Survey are among the federal agencies that employ ecologists. Other public sector opportunities are with regional, state, and local agencies. Opportunities in the private sector can be found with utilities, timber companies, and consulting firms. Some ecologists work as teachers at nature centers, middle schools and high schools, and colleges and universities.

Education and Training

Classes that will be useful include earth science, biology, ecology, chemistry, English, and math. Ecologists often use computers to

do research and record their findings. For that reason, you should also take computer science courses.

To be an ecologist you must go to college and earn a bachelor of science degree. Recommended majors are biology, botany, chemistry, ecology, geology, physics, or zoology.

You will need a master's degree for research or management jobs. If you want to work as a college teacher or research supervisor, you will need a doctoral degree.

Earnings

Salaries for ecologists vary depending on such factors as their level of education, experience, area of specialization, and the organization for which they work. Ecologists just starting out in the field might make $36,000 or less. Those with many years in the field earn $63,000 or more.

The Evolution of Ecology

The term *ecology* was first defined in 1866 by Ernst von Haeckel (1834–1919), a German biologist. He grappled with Charles Darwin's (1809–82) theory of evolution based on natural selection. This theory said that those species of plants and animals that were best adapted to their environment would survive. Haeckel did not agree with Darwin, but he and many other scientists became interested with the links between living things and their physical environment. Recognizing that there was such a link was a key step in the development of the science of ecology. The word *ecology* comes from the Greek words *oikos* (place we live) and *logos* (study of).

FOR MORE INFO

For a wide variety of publications, including *Issues in Ecology, Careers in Ecology,* and fact sheets about specific ecological concerns, contact

Ecological Society of America
1990 M Street, NW, Suite 700
Washington, DC 20036-3415
202-833-8773
esahq@esa.org
http://esa.org

For information on internships and volunteer opportunities for teens, contact

National Wildlife Federation
11100 Wildlife Center Drive

Reston, VA 20190-5362
800-822-9919
http://www.nwf.org

Contact this organization for information on volunteer positions in natural resource management for high school students.

Student Conservation Association
689 River Road
PO Box 550
Charlestown, NH 03603-0550
603-543-1700
ask-us@thesca.org
http://www.thesca.org

Outlook

The job outlook for environmental workers in general should remain good during the next decade. But there will be fewer jobs in land and water conservation. This is because so many ecologists compete for these popular jobs. Also, many environmental organizations don't have much money available to hire a large number of ecologists.

Environmental Engineers

What Environmental Engineers Do

A waste stream can be anything from wastewater, to solid waste (garbage), to hazardous waste (such as radioactive waste), to air pollution (from a factory or other source). If a private company or a city or town does not handle its waste streams properly, it can face thousands or even millions of dollars in fines from the government for breaking the law. *Environmental engineers* play an important role in controlling waste streams.

Environmental engineers may plan a sewage system, design a manufacturing plant's emissions system (which help reduce pollution), or develop a plan for a landfill site needed to bury garbage. Scientists help decide how to break down the waste. Engineers figure out how the system will work. They decide where the pipes will go, how the waste will flow through the system, and what equipment will be needed.

Environmental engineers may work for private industrial compa-

EXPLORING

- Surf the Web and check your library and bookstore for reading material on engineering and the environment.
- Volunteer for the local chapter of a nonprofit environmental organization.
- Talk to an environmental engineer about his or her career. Contact your local EPA office, check the Yellow Pages for environmental consulting firms in your area, or ask a local industrial company if you can visit.

Silent Spring Speaks Loud and Clear

The publishing of Rachel Carson's book, *Silent Spring*, in 1962 marked the beginning of the environmental movement. The well-researched book drew the public's attention to the widespread use of pesticides and their effect on the world. The title refers to Carson's belief that fewer species of birds would be singing each spring unless pesticide poisoning was stopped. Readers suddenly became aware of the amount of air, water, and soil pollution that was threatening plant, animal, and human life. The environmental movement grew and spread throughout the 1960s. In 1970, government officials set up the Environmental Protection Agency to enforce environmental protection standards, help others fight pollution, and develop and suggest new ways to protect the environment.

nies, for the Environmental Protection Agency (EPA), or for engineering consulting firms.

Environmental engineers who work for private industrial companies help make sure their companies obey environmental laws. They design new waste systems or make sure the old ones are operating correctly. Engineers might, for example, plan a system to move wastewater from the manufacturing process area to a treatment area, and then to a discharge site (a place where the treated wastewater can be pumped out). Engineers might write reports explaining the design. They also might file forms with the government to prove that the company is complying with, or obeying, the laws.

Environmental engineers who work for the EPA might not design the waste treatment systems themselves, but they do have to know how such systems are designed and built. If

DID YOU KNOW?

Where Environmental Engineers Work

- Federal government agencies such as the EPA that focus on protecting the environment
- State environmental protection agencies
- Private companies
- Engineering consulting firms
- Colleges and universities

there is a pollution problem in their area, they need to figure out if a waste control system is causing the problem, and what might have gone wrong.

Environmental engineers employed by engineering consulting firms work on many different types of problems. Consulting firms are independent companies that help others follow environmental laws. They design and build waste control systems for their clients. They also deal with the EPA on behalf of their clients. They fill out forms and check to see what requirements must be met.

Environmental engineers must like solving problems. They should enjoy science and math. They need good communication skills in order interact with people from both technical and nontechnical backgrounds. They should also be organized and have good time management skills.

Education and Training

In school, take as many science and mathematics classes as possible. It's also important to develop good communication skills, so be sure to take English and speech courses.

You will have to earn a bachelor's degree to work as an environmental engineer. About 55 colleges offer a bachelor's degree in environmental engineering. Another option is to earn another type of engineering degree such as civil, industrial, or mechanical engineering, and take additional courses in environmental engineering.

Earnings

The U.S. Department of Labor reports that average annual earnings of environmental engineers were $72,350 in 2007. Envi-

FOR MORE INFO

For information on careers, contact
American Academy of Environmental Engineers
130 Holiday Court, Suite 100
Annapolis, MD 21401-7003
410-266-3311
info@aaee.net
http://www.aaee.net

For information on environmental engineering, contact
Junior Engineering Technical Society
1420 King Street, Suite 405
Alexandria, VA 22314-2750

703-548-5387
info@jets.org
http://www.jets.org

Contact this organization for information on volunteer positions in natural resource management for high school students.
Student Conservation Association
689 River Road
PO Box 550
Charlestown, NH 03603-0550
603-543-1700
ask-us@thesca.org
http://www.thesca.org

ronmental engineers just out of college made less than $44,090. Those with a lot of experience and an advanced college degree earned $108,670 or more.

Outlook

Employment for environmental engineers will be very good in the future. Engineers will be needed to help clean up existing hazards. They will also be asked to help companies comply with government regulations. In the future, companies will ask environmental engineers to prevent problems before they happen to protect the health of the public. Jobs will be available with all three major employers—industry, the EPA, and consulting firms. The EPA has long been a big employer of environmental engineers.

Environmental Technicians

What Environmental Technicians Do

Environmental technicians test water, air, and soil for contamination by pollutants. Pollutants are harmful things such as toxic chemicals, soot, or hazardous waste that may hurt people and the environment if not eliminated or reduced. Environmental technicians work in laboratories and outdoors to find and control water, air, soil, and noise pollution. Most

EXPLORING

- Visit the Environmental Protection Agency's Web site, http://www.epa.gov/epawaste/education/teens.htm, to learn more about pollution and waste reduction.
- Read publications about environmental science and pollution control.
- Join a nature or environmental science club to learn about general issues in the field.
- Visit a health department or pollution control agency in your community. Many agencies are happy to explain their work to visitors.
- Tour a local manufacturing plant that uses air- or water-pollution control systems.

A technician collects a water sample from a watershed. Samples are collected weekly to study the effects of farming practices on water quality. (Keith Weller, U.S. Department of Agriculture, Agricultural Research Service)

environmental technicians focus on one type of pollution. Environmental technicians are sometimes called *pollution control technicians.*

Water pollution technicians collect samples of water from rivers, lakes, and other bodies of water or from wastewater. They perform chemical tests that show if it is contaminated, or polluted. In addition to testing the water, technicians may set up equipment to monitor water over a period of time to see if it is becoming polluted. Some technicians test water temperature, pressure (the strength and speed), flow, and other characteristics.

It's the Law!

As late as the 1950s, there were few environmental technicians. Environmental laws passed in the 1960s and later created the need for professionals to monitor and regulate pollution of soil, water, and air. Three of the most important environmental laws are the Clean Air Act, the Clean Water Act, and the Pollution Prevention Act.

The Clean Air Act (1970) regulates, or controls, the amount of pollution that factories and other sources can emit, or release, into the air. The act sets maximum pollutant standards, mainly for industry.

The Clean Water Act (1972) makes it against the law for individuals or companies to release pollutants into navigable waters without permission. This act aims to protect both healthy waters and restore polluted ones.

The Pollution Prevention Act (1990) encourages industry, government, and the public to reduce the amount of pollution by making better use of raw materials. The focus is on reducing the amount of waste or pollution produced in the first place, rather than trying to clean it up later.

DID YOU KNOW?

Where Environmental Technicians Work?

Water Pollution Technicians

- Manufacturers that produce wastewater
- Government agencies such as the U.S. Environmental Protection Agency (EPA) and the U.S. Departments of Agriculture, Energy, and Interior
- Municipal wastewater treatment facilities
- Private firms that monitor or control pollutants in water or wastewater

Air Pollution Technicians

- Manufacturers that produce airborne pollutants
- Government agencies such as the EPA and the U.S. Departments of Agriculture, Energy, and Interior
- Research facilities
- Pollution control equipment manufacturers

Soil Pollution Technicians

- Federal or state departments of agriculture
- U.S. EPA and state EPAs
- U.S. Department of Agriculture
- Private organizations that monitor soil quality for pesticide levels

Noise Pollution Technicians

- Private companies that have processes that produce a lot of noise
- Government agencies such as the Occupational Safety and Health Administration

Air pollution technicians collect and analyze samples of gas emissions (smoke) and the atmosphere. They try to find out how badly exhaust fumes from automobiles are polluting the air, or whether the smoke from industrial plants contains hazardous pollution. They often set up monitoring equipment outdoors to take air samples, or they may try to create the same conditions in a laboratory.

Soil or *land pollution technicians* collect soil, silt, or mud samples so they can be checked for contamination. Soil can be contaminated when polluted water or waste seeps into the earth.

Noise pollution technicians use rooftop devices and mobile units to check noise levels of factories, highways, airports, and other places. Some test noise levels of construction equipment, chain saws, lawn mowers, or other equipment. High noise levels can harm workers and the public.

Environmental technicians should be curious, patient, detail-oriented, and able to follow instructions. They need basic manual skills in order to collect samples and perform tests in laboratories. They should also be comfortable using computers and testing equipment. Environmental technicians must be able to keep accurate and detailed records and be in good physical condition.

Education and Training

Pollution control is highly technical work. You will need to take as many mathematics (algebra and geometry) and laboratory science (chemistry, physics, and biology) courses as you can in high school. Communications, computer science, conservation, and ecology classes are also important.

After high school, you need to complete a two-year program in environmental technology. These programs are offered at community and junior colleges, and at technical schools. Some employers also offer on-the-job training for new employees.

Earnings

Pay for environmental technicians varies widely depending on the nature of the work they do, training and experience required for the work, type of employer, geographic region, and other factors.

According to the U.S. Department of Labor, the average annual salary for environmental science and protection tech-

FOR MORE INFO

For information on environmental careers and degree programs, contact
Advanced Technology Environmental and Energy Center
500 Belmont Road
Bettendorf, IA 52722-5649
http://www.ateec.org

For information on careers and a list of colleges that offer environmental degrees, contact
Air and Waste Management Association
420 Fort Duquesne Boulevard
One Gateway Center, Third Floor
Pittsburgh, PA 15222-1435
412-232-3444
info@awma.org
http://www.awma.org

For information on environmental careers, resources and activities for young people, and volunteer opportunities for high school students, contact
U.S. Environmental Protection Agency
Ariel Rios Building
1200 Pennsylvania Avenue, NW
Washington, DC 20004-2403
202-272-0167
http://www.epa.gov/kids

For information on water and sanitation, contact
Water Environment Federation
601 Wythe Street
Alexandria, VA 22314-1994
800-666-0206
http://www.wef.org

nicians was $39,370 in 2007. Salaries ranged from less than $25,090 (new workers) to more than $63,670 (experienced workers). Technicians who worked for local governments earned average salaries of $45,390 in 2007. Those who worked for state governments earned $45,050. Environmental technicians employed by colleges and universities earned $43,120. Technicians who become managers or supervisors can earn $70,000 per year or more. Technicians who work in private industry or who further their education to secure teaching positions can also expect to earn higher-than-average salaries.

Outlook

There should be many new jobs for environmental technicians in the future. They will be needed to collect soil, water, and air samples to measure pollution levels. There will also be many positions available for technicians to clean up contaminated sites and make sure that private companies follow environmental laws. The demand for environmental technicians should continue due to public concern for the environment.

There will be jobs available wherever there are many factories and strict state and local pollution control laws. As long as the federal government supports pollution control, the environmental control industry will continue to grow.

Fish and Game Wardens

What Fish and Game Wardens Do

Fish and game wardens protect wildlife, manage resources, teach the public, and make sure that environmental laws are followed. They are also called *wildlife conservationists, wildlife inspectors, refuge rangers,* and *refuge officers.*

The conservation, or protection, of fish and wildlife is a task that grows more complex each year. Increasing pollution and

EXPLORING

- Visit your local nature centers and park preserves often. Attend any classes or special lectures that are available. There may be opportunities to volunteer to help clean up sites, plant trees, or maintain pathways and trails.
- Get to know your local wildlife. What kind of insects, birds, fish, and other animals live in your area? Are any threatened or endangered? Visit the U.S. Fish and Wildlife Service's Web site, http://www.fws.gov, for a list.
- Interview a fish and game warden about his or her career. Ask the following questions: What made you want to enter the field? What do you like most and least about your job?, How did you train to become a fish and game warden?, What advice would you give to someone who is interested in the career?

changes in the environment are putting many animals at risk. To accomplish its mission, the U.S. Fish and Wildlife Service, for example, employs many of the country's best biologists, wildlife managers, engineers, and law enforcement agents. These professionals work to save endangered and threatened species and conserve migratory birds and inland fisheries. They also provide expert advice to other federal agencies, industry, and foreign governments and manage more than 700 offices and field stations. These personnel work in every state and territory—from the Arctic Ocean to the South Pacific, and from the Atlantic to the Caribbean.

Wildlife inspectors and *special agents* are two jobs that fall in the fish and game warden category of the U.S. Fish and Wildlife Service. Wildlife inspectors monitor the legal trade of federally protected fish and wildlife and intercept, or stop, illegal imports and exports. Some animals are so rare that it is against the law to hunt them or bring them into (import) or take them out of (export) the United States. At points of entry into the United States,

The National Wildlife Refuge System

The National Wildlife Refuge System (http://www.fws.gov/refuges) is a system of public lands and waters set aside "to conserve America's fish, wildlife and plants." The 96 million-acre system includes

- more than 700 species of birds, 250 reptile and amphibian species, 220 species of mammals, and more than 200 species of fish
- 550 national wildlife refuges
- thousands of smaller wetlands and other special management areas
- 66 national fish hatcheries
- 64 fishery resource offices
- 78 ecological services field stations

wildlife inspectors examine shipping containers, live animals, wildlife products such as animal skins, and documents. Inspectors, who work closely with special agents, may seize shipments as evidence, conduct investigations, and testify in courts of law.

Special agents of the U.S. Fish and Wildlife Service are trained criminal investigators who enforce federal wildlife laws throughout the country. Special agents conduct investigations, which may include surveillance (observing people to see if they are breaking the law), undercover work, making arrests, and preparing cases for court. These agents enforce migratory bird regulations and investigate illegal trade in protected wildlife.

Refuge rangers or refuge managers work at 550 national refuges across the country. They help protect and conserve migratory and native species of birds, mammals, fish, endangered species, and other wildlife. Many of these refuges also offer outdoor recreational opportunities and educational programs.

> ## Tips for Success
>
> To be a successful fish and game warden, you should
>
> - be in good physical condition
> - enjoy being outdoors
> - want to help protect the environment
> - be willing to travel for job assignments
> - have good communication skills
> - be firm when dealing with law breakers

Education and Training

Courses in biology and other sciences, geography, mathematics, social studies, and physical education will help you prepare for this career.

To become a fish and game warden you must have a bachelor's degree or three years of work experience. Higher positions require at least one year of graduate studies. Some professional

FOR MORE INFO

You can learn more about fish and game wardens and related employment opportunities by contacting the following organizations:

National Park Service
U.S. Department of the Interior
1849 C Street, NW
Washington, DC 20240-0001
202-208-6843
http://www.nps.gov

U.S. Fish and Wildlife Service
U.S. Department of the Interior
4401 North Fairfax Drive
Arlington, VA 22203-1610
800-344-WILD
http://www.fws.gov

positions, such as biologist or manager, require master's or doctoral degrees.

On-the-job training is given for most positions. Special agents receive 18 weeks of formal training in criminal investigation and wildlife law enforcement techniques at the Federal Law Enforcement Training Center in Glynco, Georgia.

Earnings

In the wide variety of positions available at the U.S. Fish and Wildlife Service, salaries range from $21,000 for new workers up to $149,000 for more advanced positions. Law enforcement workers, especially special agents, receive higher salaries than support workers because their jobs are more dangerous.

Outlook

There will always be a need for fish and game wardens to protect natural resources. The largest number of jobs in the field are with the U.S. Fish and Wildlife Service and the National Park Service. State agencies, such as departments of natural resources or departments of parks and recreation, also offer jobs.

Employment growth in this field depends on politics and government. Some presidents and governors spend more on wildlife concerns, while others make cutbacks in this area. When funding is available, there are more opportunities for fish and game wardens. When funding is cut, fish and game warden positions may be eliminated or agencies may hire fewer workers.

Foresters

What Foresters Do

Foresters protect and manage forests. They plant trees, control diseases or insects, scatter seeds, and prune, or cut, trees. They map the locations of resources, such as timber, places animals rest, food, snow, and water. Foresters lay out logging roads or

EXPLORING

- Read about trees and forests. Learn the names and types of trees and plants in forests. Here are some tree resources to explore: *The Illustrated Encyclopedia of Trees of the World,* by Catherine Cutler, Tony Russell, and Martin Walters (Lorenz Books, 2007); *National Geographic Field Guide to Trees of North America,* by Keith Rushforth and Charles Hollis (National Geographic, 2006); and *Trees: A Visual Guide,* by Tony Rodd and Jennifer Stackhouse (University of California Press, 2008).

- Visit the Web sites of colleges and universities that offer programs in forestry. Visit http://www.safnet.org for a list of programs.
- Visit forest preserves in your area. Most preserves offer educational programs and workshops. Some have volunteer programs.
- In some parts of the country, local chapters of the Society of American Foresters invite students who are interested in forestry to some of their meetings and field trips (see For More Info).

roads to lakes and campgrounds. Some foresters create the plans for building campgrounds and shelters, supervise work crews, and inspect the work after it is done.

Fires often damage or destroy forests. To help prevent forest fires, foresters select and mark dead or diseased trees to be cut. They may use controlled burns to reduce brush that may fuel dangerous wildfires. (When a large amount of dead plants and trees build up on the forest floor, there is a major risk that a fire could start and destroy the forest and even threaten the lives of people who live nearby. A controlled burn is a planned low-intensity fire that is set by professionals to reduce the chance of a larger fire destroying the forest.) They are in charge of the lookouts, patrols, and pilots who watch for fires. They also lead crews that fight fires. Some foresters supervise campgrounds, find lost hikers, and rescue climbers and skiers. Foresters must record the work done in the forest on maps and in reports. Sometimes they use computers and data processing equipment. They also use aerial photography. Some foresters work in the laboratories and factories of wood-related industries, such as sawmills, pulp and paper mills, wood preserving plants, and furniture factories. Others do research in laboratories, green-houses, and forests.

Foresters may specialize. For example, *silviculturists* specialize in the establishment and reproduction of forests. They regulate the types and numbers of trees and plants that are in a forest, and manage forest growth and development. *Forest ecologists* study how forests are affected by changes in environmental conditions, such as light, soil, climate, altitude, and animals. *Urban foresters* live and work in urban areas. They oversee trees and related ecosystems (a group of organisms living together with nonliving components) in forests and woodlands, as well as those on city streets. *Conservation education foresters* teach students and educators about the proper care and management of forests. *Forest engineers* design and construct roads, bridges, dams, and buildings in forest areas.

These construction projects help the movement of logs and pulpwood out of the forest.

Foresters need to have excellent scientific knowledge. They should be curious, enjoy solving problems, and have a strong love of the outdoors. They also should be in good physical shape and enjoy physical activity.

Education and Training

To prepare for this field, take as many math and science courses as possible in school. Take algebra, geometry, and statistics as well as biology, chemistry, physics, and any science courses that will teach you about ecology and forestry. English classes are also important to take since part of your job is likely to include research, writing reports, and presenting your findings. In addition, take history, economics, and, if

Forest Facts

- It has been estimated that Americans come in contact with more than 10,000 items each day that come from forests.
- Most forest fires are now detected by aircraft or closed-circuit television, rather than the traditional lookout towers.
- The largest forest area in the United States is the Central Hardwood Forest. It stretches across eastern North America and encompasses part or all of 28 U.S. states and two Canadian provinces.
- Most hardwoods are deciduous. This means they lose their leaves each fall. Most softwoods are evergreens, which means they lose only some of their needles each year and remain green year-round.
- Older, slower-growing trees and trees that have been damaged by fire or drought are most likely to be attacked by disease and insects.

DID YOU KNOW?

Where Foresters Work

- Federal government agencies such as the Forest Service, the Bureau of Land Management, and the National Park Service
- State and local agencies
- Private companies (logging and lumber companies, saw-mills, and research and testing facilities)
- Self-employment

possible, agriculture classes, which will teach you about soils and plant growth, among other things.

A professional forester must graduate from a four-year school of forestry with a bachelor's degree. Some foresters have master's degrees. Most schools of forestry are part of state universities. In forestry school, you learn how to manage forests and make them healthy. You work in the forest as a part of your university training.

Earnings

According to the U.S. Department of Labor, median annual earnings of foresters were $52,440 in 2007. New foresters might earn less than $34,000. Very experienced workers make more than $76,000 a year.

In 2006, most bachelor's degree graduates entering the federal government as foresters earned $28,862 to $35,752, depending on their grades in school. Those with a master's degree started at $43,731 to $52,912, and those with doctorates started at $63,417. In 2007, foresters working for the federal government earned an average salary of $65,964.

Outlook

Job opportunities in forestry are expected to grow more slowly than the average for all careers. Budget cuts in federal programs have limited hiring. Also, federal land management agencies, such as the Forest Service, are giving less attention to timber programs and are focusing more on stopping wildfires, law enforcement, wildlife management, recreation, and

FOR MORE INFO

For information on forestry and forests in the United States, contact
American Forests
PO Box 2000
Washington, DC 20013-2000
202-737-1944
info@amfor.org
http://www.americanforests.org

For information on forests, forestry careers, and schools, contact
Society of American Foresters
5400 Grosvenor Lane
Bethesda, MD 20814-2198
866-897-8720
safweb@safnet.org
http://www.safnet.org

For information on urban forestry, contact
Society of Municipal Arborists
http://www.urban-forestry.com

For information about government careers in forestry and national forests across the country, contact
U.S. Forest Service
U.S. Department of Agriculture
1400 Independence Avenue, SW
Washington, DC 20250-0003
800-832-1355
http://www.fs.fed.us

taking care of ecosystems. This development is good for environmentalist workers in general, but may create fewer jobs for foresters and more openings for people in other environmental careers.

Geologists

What Geologists Do

Geologists study the earth—how it was formed, what it is made of, and how it is slowly changing. They gather rocks to study. Generally, geologists spend three to six months of the year making maps of certain areas and drilling deep holes in the earth to obtain these rock samples. They study the rock samples in their laboratories under controlled temperatures and pressures. Finally, they organize the information they have gathered and write reports. These reports may be used to find groundwater, oil, minerals, and other natural resources.

Many geologists focus on a particular study of the earth. For example, those who study the oceans are called *marine*

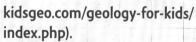

EXPLORING

- Visit Web sites about geology, such as Schoolyard Geology (http://education.usgs.gov/schoolyard), Kidipede: Geology for Kids (http://www.history-forkids.org/scienceforkids/geology/index.htm), and KidsGeo.com (http://www.

kidsgeo.com/geology-for-kids/index.php).
- Amateur geological groups and local museums may have geology clubs you can join.
- Ask your science teacher or guidance counselor to arrange an information interview with a geologist.

geologists. Those who try to locate natural gas and oil deposits are called *petroleum geologists. Paleontologists* study the earth's rock formations to determine the age of the earth. *Engineering geologists* use their knowledge of geology to help solve problems that come up during the construction of roads, buildings, bridges, dams, and other structures. *Petrologists* study the origin and composition of igneous, metamorphic, and sedimentary rocks. *Stratigraphers* study the distribution and arrangement of sedimentary rock layers. This helps them to understand evolutionary changes in fossils and plants. *Geohydrologists* study the nature and distribution of water within the earth. They often take part in studies that assess how a construction project will affect the environment. *Geomorphologists* study the form of the earth's surface and the processes, such as erosion and glaciation, that bring about changes. *Volcanologists* study volcanoes, their location, and their activity.

DID YOU KNOW?

Where Geologists Work

- Oil and gas companies and other private businesses
- Federal government agencies including the Department of the Interior (the U.S. Geological Survey, National Park Service, and the Bureau of Reclamation) and in the Departments of Defense, Agriculture, and Commerce
- State and local government agencies
- Research organizations
- Colleges and universities
- Museums

The work of geologists can be demanding. They travel often to remote and rugged sites by helicopter or four-wheel drive vehicle and walk long distances. They may camp for extended periods of time in rough conditions away from their families. In addition, they spend long hours in the laboratory and preparing reports.

In addition to scientific skills, geologists should have good communication skills, be organized, be able to think independently and creatively, and have physical stamina to do fieldwork.

Education and Training

Take a college preparatory curriculum while in high school. Such a curriculum will include computer science, history, English, and geography classes. Science and math classes are also important to take, particularly earth science, chemistry,

Types of Rocks

There are three types of rocks: igneous, sedimentary, and metamorphic.

Igneous rocks are created by the cooling and hardening of magma (molten rock that is located deep inside the earth). They are found often on the earth's surface as a result of being expelled from beneath the ground by volcanoes. These types of rocks are called extrusive igneous rocks. Some igneous rocks remain just below the surface (they are called intrusive igneous rocks). Examples of igneous rocks are obsidian and basalt.

Sedimentary rocks are made up of small pieces of rock, sand, shells, and other materials that are pushed together and cemented to one another. Sedimentary rock is often made up soft layers. It is the only type of rock that contain fossils. Examples of sedimentary rocks are amber, sandstone, anthracite, and limestone

Metamorphic rocks change their properties because of alterations in temperature or pressure. They are formed underground. These rocks often have ribbon-like layers and sometimes have crystals. Any rock can change into a metamorphic rock if it is exposed to these conditions. Examples of metamorphic rocks are slate and marble.

With the main crater and lava dome of Washington's Mount St. Helens behind them, U.S. Geological Survey geologists set up a GPS device. (Ted S. Warren, AP Images)

and physics. Math classes should include algebra, trigonometry, and statistics.

To be a geologist, you need to earn a bachelor's degree, usually in the physical and earth sciences. Positions in research, teaching, or exploration require a master's degree. Geologists who want to teach in a college or university or head a department in a business must earn a doctorate.

Many colleges, universities, and technical institutes offer programs in geology. Besides courses in geology, students study

FOR MORE INFO

For information on geoscience careers, contact
American Geological Institute
4220 King Street
Alexandria, VA 22302-1502
703-379-2480
http://www.agiweb.org

For information on careers, contact
American Institute of Professional Geologists
1400 West 122nd Avenue, Suite 250
Westminster, CO 80234-3499
303-412-6205

aipg@aipg.org
http://www.aipg.org

For career information, contact
Geological Society of America
PO Box 9140
Boulder, CO 80301-9140
888-443-4472
gsaservice@geosociety.org
http://www.geosociety.org

For career and educational information about the geosciences, visit
U.S. Geological Survey
http://www.usgs.gov/education

physics, chemistry, mathematics, English composition, economics, and foreign languages. Students who go on to graduate school will take advanced courses in geology and in the specialization of their choice.

The U.S. Department of Labor reports that the average annual salary for geoscientists was $75,800 in 2007. New geologists earned $41,000 or less. Experienced geologists with advanced degrees earned more than $144,000. In the federal government, the average salary for geologists was $88,820 a year in 2007. Geologists who worked for state governments earned about $60,000 in 2008.

Outlook

Employment opportunities for geologists should be very good. Geologists will find jobs in the petroleum industry, but competition for those positions will be strong. Many of these jobs may be in foreign countries. Geologists may also find jobs in environmental protection and reclamation (cleanup). Those with master's degrees who are familiar with computer modeling and the Global Positioning System will have the best employment opportunities. Knowing a foreign language will also help you land a job.

Land Acquisition Professionals

What Land Acquisition Professionals Do

Land trusts are private nonprofit groups formed to acquire, or obtain, lands and manage them for the public's benefit. *Land acquisition professionals* handle the transactions needed to acquire the land or rights to the land.

Trustees of Reservations, the first U.S. land trust, was formed in Boston in 1891. Concerned about development of

EXPLORING

- To learn more about this career, read publications such as the Land Trust Alliance's book *Starting a Land Trust*. Although this book is written for adults, browsing its pages will give you a general idea of the issues you will encounter if you decide to work in the field.
- Contact the large national land trust organizations for career information.

- Try to get involved with a land trust organization near you. The large national organizations should be able to provide you with the names of local groups.
- Ask your school counselor to arrange an information interview with a land acquisition professional.

lands around the city, this group bought up some land itself and opened it to the public. Today, there are more than 1,665 trusts nationwide. They range from small, one-person trusts, to large state trusts, to national organizations that help out the smaller trusts.

Land acquisitions may be someone's entire job or just one of many duties. An executive director for a small land trust, for example, may do everything from acquiring the land to managing it on a day-to-day basis. Larger, well-funded trusts and the national organizations may employ one or more people who do nothing but work on acquisitions.

There are many reasons for choosing a site to save. The trust may want to stop overly heavy grazing, farming, or recreation on the land. It may want to keep open lands from being bought by a developer. It may want the rights to a pond or lake to clean it up and bring back native wildlife. Some trusts specialize in finding, buying, and managing lands with rare or endangered species.

After the site is picked, the acquisitions professional finds out who owns the site, contacts them, and attempts to convince them to sell or donate it. There are certain tax advantages, or benefits, for donating the land. Most trusts are nonprofit organizations, and donations to them are tax deductible. If the owner leaves the land to the trust in his or her will, this, too, can bring tax advantages. This means that

DID YOU KNOW?

- There were more than 1,665 land trusts in the United States.
- Approximately 37 million acres were conserved—an area 16.5 times the size of Yellowstone National Park.
- The Western U.S. had the most (44 percent) land trusts, followed by the Northeast (30 percent), Mid-Atlantic (14 percent), Southeast (8 percent), and Midwest (4 percent).
- California, Maine, Colorado, Montana, Virginia, New York, Vermont, New Mexico, Pennsylvania, and Massachusetts had the highest total acres conserved in land trusts.

Source: 2005 National Land Trust Census

if they put the land in a trust, they may be able to pay lower taxes to the government.

If the owner will not donate the land, the acquisitions professional tries to persuade him or her to sell it. The trust needs to go through a legal process to officially obtain the rights to the land. The process is similar to buying a house or other real estate.

Land trusts exist across the nation. Work with a large national organization might involve travel to help smaller land trusts.

Education and Training

To prepare for a career in this field, take business, economics, and English courses in high school. It is also a good idea to take as many science courses as you can, such as biology and earth science. Try to land a volunteer position or an internship with a local land trust. Although you will probably just do clerical work, you will gain valuable on-the-job experience and be able to observe land acquisition professionals as they do their work.

Negotiating skills are more important to an acquisitions professional than any specific schooling or work background. Communication skills are also important.

Land trusts employ people from different types of educational backgrounds, from scientists to accountants. Real estate backgrounds may be useful for people wanting to focus on acquisitions work.

Tips for Success

To be a successful land acquisition professional, you should

- be hard working and dedicated to the field of land conservation
- have good communication skills
- be organized and able to handle multiple tasks
- be a good negotiator
- have knowledge of land conservation options and techniques
- be skilled in business administration, finance, and law

FOR MORE INFO

The following is a national organization of more than 1,665 land trusts nationwide:

Land Trust Alliance
1660 L Street, NW, Suite 1100
Washington, DC 20036-5635
202-638-4725
info@lta.org
http://www.lta.org

The following organization specializes in land trusts and land trust management for areas with rare or endangered species. For information about internships with TNC state chapters or at TNC headquarters, contact

The Nature Conservancy (TNC)
4245 North Fairfax Drive, Suite 100
Arlington, VA 22203-1606
703-841-5300
comment@tnc.org
http://www.nature.org

Contact this organization for information on volunteer positions in natural resource management for high school students.

Student Conservation Association
689 River Road
PO Box 550
Charlestown, NH 03603-0550
603-543-1700
ask-us@thesca.org
http://www.thesca.org

For information on land conservation careers, contact

The Trust for Public Land
116 New Montgomery Street,
Fourth Floor
San Francisco, CA 94105-3638
800-714-LAND
info@tpl.org
http://www.tpl.org

However, most acquisitions professionals are trained on the job. Land acquisitions professionals have bachelor's degrees in a wide variety of fields, including law, city planning, journalism, and real estate.

Earnings

Less than half of the land trusts have paid staff. However, executive directors of land trusts may earn salaries that range from $35,000 to $80,000 or more annually. Acquisitions professionals employed by national groups may earn $60,000 or more per year.

Outlook

The outlook for land trust work currently is brighter than that for federal land and water conservation jobs. Land trusts are going strong right now, and the entire land and water conservation segment, of which land trust and preserve management is a part, is growing at a steady rate annually.

Land acquisition professionals with advanced degrees and, most importantly, experience working at one of the larger land trusts will have the best employment prospects.

Land Trust or Preserve Managers

What Land Trust or Preserve Managers Do

Land that is especially beautiful, has rare animals living on it, or is special in other ways is often kept from being developed (or built up), polluted, mined, too heavily farmed, or otherwise damaged. This type of protection is called a land trust or preserve. Hundreds of millions of acres of land and water are protected in this way. Land trusts and preserves are owned by private organizations, preserves, and the government.

Land trust and preserve managers plan for recreational use of land and water, such as hiking or camping. They count the plant and animal species and protect wildlife habitats. They clean up pollution and restore damaged ecosystems (a group of nonliving and living components). They manage forests, prairies, rangelands, and wetlands using techniques such as controlled burnings and grazing by bison or cattle.

Land trust managers work for private, nonprofit land trusts. Land

EXPLORING

- Ask your librarian to help you find books on prairie, wetland, riparian (river bank), and wildlife conservation, as well as land trusts and preservation.
- Contact nonprofit land trusts (such as The Nature Conservancy) or federal agencies for information about current projects in your area.
- Ask your guidance counselor or science teacher to arrange an information interview with a land trust or preserve manager.

trusts have become an important way for people who care about the environment to take action. For example, in the 1970s, a land trust saved miles of San Francisco coastline from development. Land trusts get land by buying it, accepting it as a donation, or purchasing the development rights to it. There are more than 1,665 land trusts in the United States today. Land trusts can be small; one person might do everything. A few land trusts have a large, paid staff of 30 or more.

Preserve managers work for the federal government, which owns more than 700 million acres, about one-third of the United States, including forests, wilderness areas, wildlife refuges, scenic rivers, and other sites. Most of this land is managed by agencies, such as the National Park Service, U.S. Fish and Wildlife Service, Bureau of Land Management, and U.S. Forest Service. State and local governments also may own and manage preserve lands.

Teddy Roosevelt and the Environment

One of the most important people in early conservation efforts was Theodore Roosevelt, the 26th president of the United States. Roosevelt fell in love with the West (areas that are west of the Mississippi River) as a young man, when illness led him there to seek better air. He owned a ranch in the Dakota Territory (what is now North and South Dakota) and wrote many books about his experiences in the West.

When he became president in 1901, Roosevelt used his influence to help preserve his beloved West. He promoted conservation as part of an overall strategy for the responsible use of natural resources, including forests, pastures, fish, game, soil, and minerals. His efforts increased public awareness of and support for conservation. They also led to important early conservation legislation. Roosevelt's administration especially emphasized the preservation of forests, wildlife, park lands, wilderness areas, and watershed areas and carried out such work as the first inventory of natural resources in this country.

The federal government employs about 75 percent of all people working in land and water conservation.

Land trust and preserve managers must be dedicated to the field of land conservation. They also need the ability to speak and write clearly. They have to be able to juggle many tasks at once and have good people skills in order to work with people from different backgrounds. Land trust and preserve managers who manage the business aspects of their organization should have skills in business administration, finance, and law.

DID YOU KNOW?

Land trusts are the fastest-growing segment of the conservation movement today, with approximately 1,667 in 2005, according to the Land Trust Alliance (LTA). The LTA's National Land Trust Census reports that local, state, and national land trusts protected 37 million acres as of 2005—an increase of 54 percent from 2000.

Education and Training

If you are interested in scientific work take biology, chemistry, physics, botany, and ecology classes. All potential land trust or preserve managers can benefit from courses in business, computer science, English, and speech.

A background in biology, chemistry, and physics is important for land trust or preserve managers. A bachelor's degree in a natural science, such as zoology, biology, or botany, is recommended. A master's or a doctorate in a specialty also is a good idea, especially for government positions.

Land trusts need people who are good in business to run the trusts, raise funds, negotiate deals, and handle tax matters. The large land trust organizations also need lawyers, public relations specialists, and others.

Earnings

According to the National Association of Colleges and Employers, graduates with a bachelor's degree in environmental

FOR MORE INFO

The following is a national organization of more than 1,665 land trusts nationwide.

Land Trust Alliance
1660 L Street, NW, Suite 1100
Washington, DC 20036-5635
202-638-4725
info@lta.org
http://www.lta.org

The following organization specializes in land trusts and land trust management for areas with rare or endangered species. For information about internships with TNC state chapters or at TNC headquarters, contact

The Nature Conservancy (TNC)
4245 North Fairfax Drive, Suite 100
Arlington, VA 22203-1606
703-841-5300
comment@tnc.org
http://www.nature.org

Contact this organization for information on volunteer positions in natural resource management for high school students.

Student Conservation Association
689 River Road
PO Box 550
Charlestown, NH 03603-0550
603-543-1700
ask-us@thesca.org
http://www.thesca.org

For information on land conservation careers, contact

The Trust for Public Land
116 New Montgomery Street,
Fourth Floor
San Francisco, CA 94105-3638
800-714-LAND
info@tpl.org
http://www.tpl.org

science received average starting salaries of $38,336 in 2007. Earnings for conservation workers ranged from less than $32,000 to $82,000 or more annually. Conservation professionals with master's degrees and experience earn higher salaries.

Outlook

Land trusts are growing in popularity. Currently, private land trusts and national land trust organizations offer the most jobs. Employment is expected to be slow with federal land trusts. Those who have both environmental and business training will have the best job prospects.

Naturalists

What Naturalists Do

Naturalists study the natural world. They do so in order to learn the best way to preserve the earth and its living creatures—humans, animals, and plants. They teach the public about the environment and show people what they can do about such hazards as pollution.

Naturalists also can work as *nature resource managers, wildlife conservationists, ecologists,* and *environmental educators* for many different employers.

Depending on where they work, naturalists may protect and conserve wildlife or particular kinds of land, such as prairie or wetlands. Other naturalists research and carry out plans to restore lands that have been damaged by erosion (the wearing away of soil and other land features by water, wind, and human activities), fire, or development (the building of homes, highways, and other structures). Some naturalists recreate wildlife habitats and nature trails. They plant trees, for

EXPLORING

- Read books and magazines about nature and a career as a naturalist.
- Visit your local nature centers and park preserves often. Attend any classes or special lectures they offer. There may be opportunities to volunteer to help clean up sites, plant trees, or maintain pathways and trails.
- Hiking, birdwatching, and photography are good hobbies for future naturalists.
- Get to know your local wildlife. What kind of insects, birds, fish, and other animals live in your area? Your librarian will be able to help you find books that identify local flora and fauna.

DID YOU KNOW?

Where Naturalists Work

- Wildlife museums
- Private nature centers
- Large zoos
- Parks and nature preserves
- Arboretums
- Botanical gardens
- Government agencies such as the U.S. Fish and Wildlife Service or the National Park Service

example, or label existing plants (so hikers and campers know what they are). *Fish and wildlife wardens* help manage populations of fish, hunted animals, and protected animals. They control hunting and fishing and make sure species are thriving but not overpopulating their territories. Overpopulation happens when too many of one type of plant or animal takes over an area. *Wildlife managers, range managers,* and *conservationists* also maintain the plant and animal life in a certain area. They work in parks or on ranges that have both domestic livestock (animals such as cattle that have been tamed by humans) and wild animals (such as deer, bears, and coyotes). They test soil and water for pollution and nutrients (substances that encourage growth). They count plant and animal populations each season.

Naturalists also work indoors. They raise money for projects, write reports, keep detailed records, and write articles, brochures, and newsletters to tell the public about their work. They might campaign for support for protection of an endangered species by holding meetings and hearings. (An endangered species is an organism that has so few individual survivors that it may become extinct.) Other public education activities include leading tours and nature walks and holding demonstrations, exhibits, and classes.

Naturalists should enjoy working outdoors since they spend the majority of their time outside in all kinds of weather. They should also be able to work well with other environmental professionals and the general public. They should be good teachers in order to educate the public about nature and environmental issues. Finally, naturalists should have good writing skills in order to prepare educational materials and grant proposals.

A naturalist talks about an eastern screech owl during a presentation for school children. (Stephen Lance Dennee, The Paducah Sun/AP Images)

Education and Training

If you are interested in this field, you should take basic science courses in high school, including biology, chemistry, and earth science. Botany courses and clubs are also helpful, since they will give you direct experience observing plant growth and health.

Naturalists must have at least a bachelor's degree in biology, zoology, chemistry, botany, natural history, or environmental science. A master's degree is not required, but is helpful. Many naturalists have a master's degree in education. Experience gained through summer jobs and volunteer work can be just as important as educational requirements. Experience working with the public is also helpful.

Earnings

Starting salaries for full-time naturalists range from about $20,000 to $29,000 per year. Some part-time workers, however, earn as little as minimum wage ($7.25 per hour). For some positions, housing and vehicles may be provided. Earnings vary for those with more responsibilities or advanced degrees. The U.S. Department of Labor reports that conservation scientists (a career category that includes naturalists) earned an average annual salary of $56,150 in 2007. Experienced naturalists made $82,080 or more.

The Young Naturalist Awards

If you are in grades seven through 12, you can participate in The Young Naturalist Awards—a competition that is held by the American Museum of Natural History. To compete, you need to "plan and conduct your own scientific investigation, one that will include questions, hypotheses, and trips into the field to gather data." No one is expecting you to make a new scientific discovery. Instead, your investigation should help you better understand a part of the natural world. Sample questions might include: How many trees are in my neighborhood? Is our local creek polluted? What do leopard frogs like to eat? Or, When do deer sleep? You compete for the award by writing an essay about your research and the results of your investigation. You can also include photos that show your work. This contest is a great way to develop your scientific skills and explore the world around you. Winners receive a cash prize. Visit http://www.amnh.org/nationalcenter/youngnaturalistaward to learn more about this exciting contest and to read past winning essays.

FOR MORE INFO

For information on careers, contact
American Society of Naturalists
http://www.amnat.org

For information about career opportunities, contact
Bureau of Land Management
U.S. Department of the Interior
1849 C Street
Washington, DC 20240-0001
http://www.blm.gov

For information on conservation programs, contact
National Wildlife Federation
11100 Wildlife Center Drive
Reston, VA 20190-5362
800-822-9919
http://www.nwf.org

For information on conservation and volunteer opportunities, contact
Student Conservation Association
689 River Road
PO Box 550
Charlestown, NH 03603-0550
603-543-1700
ask-us@thesca.org
http://www.thesca.org

For information on careers, contact
U.S. Fish and Wildlife Service
U.S. Department of the Interior
4401 North Fairfax Drive
Arlington, VA 22203-1610
http://www.fws.gov/jobs

Outlook

In the next decade, the job outlook for naturalists is expected to be only fair, despite the public's increasing interest in the environment. Private nature centers and preserves—where forests, wetlands, and prairies are restored—are continuing to open in the United States. But possible government cutbacks in the amount of money provided to nature programs may limit their growth. Many people want to enter this field, which will make it difficult to land a job.

Oceanographers

What Oceanographers Do

Oceanographers study the oceans. They conduct experiments and gather information about the water, plant and animal life, and the ocean floor. They study the motion of waves, currents (a strong flow of water in an ocean or lake), and tides (the regular rise and fall of ocean water). They also look at water temperature,

EXPLORING

- Visit Web sites that focus on oceanography. Interesting sites include Careers in Oceanography, Marine Science, and Marine Biology (http://ocean.peterbrueggeman.com/career.html), MarineBio.org (http://www.marinebio.com), and Sea Grant Marine Careers (http://www.marinecareers.net).

- If you live near coastal regions, it will be easier to learn about oceans and ocean life. Read all you can about rocks, minerals, and aquatic life. If you live or travel near an oceanography research center, such as Woods Hole Oceanographic Institution (http://www.whoi.edu) on Cape Cod in Massachusetts, spend some time studying its exhibits.

- If you do not live near water, try to find summer camps or programs that make trips to coastal areas. Learn all you can about the geology, atmosphere, and plant and animal life of the area where you live, regardless of whether water is present.

chemical makeup of the ocean water, oil deposits on the ocean floor, and pollution levels at different depths of the oceans.

Oceanographers use several inventions specially designed for long- and short-term underwater observation. They use deep-sea equipment, such as submarines and observation tanks. Underwater devices called bathyspheres allow an oceanographer to stay underwater for several hours or even days. For short observations or to explore areas such as underwater caves, scientists use deep-sea and scuba diving gear that straps onto the body to supply them with oxygen.

Oceanographers do most of their work out on the water. While at sea, they gather the scientific information that they need. Then they spend months or years in offices, laboratories, or libraries studying the data. Oceanographers use information such as water temperature changes between the surface and the lower depths to predict droughts and monsoon rains. Droughts are periods of time when there is little or no rain. Monsoon rains are heavy rains that can cause major flooding and damage.

Most oceanographers specialize in one of four areas.

Those who study ocean plants and animals are called *biological oceanographers* or *marine biologists.* They collect information on the behavior and activities of the wildlife in a specific area of the ocean.

Physical oceanographers study ocean temperature and the atmosphere above the water. They study the greenhouse effect, or the warming of the planet's surface. They calculate the movement of the warm water (known as a current) through the oceans to help meteorologists predict weather patterns.

Geological oceanographers study the ocean floor. They use instruments that monitor the ocean floor and the minerals found there from a far distance. In areas where the ocean is too deep for any man-made equipment to go, they use remote sensors.

Geochemical oceanographers study the chemical makeup of ocean water and the ocean floor. They detect oil well sites. They

Helping Hands: Jacques-Yves Cousteau

Jacques-Yves Cousteau was a world famous oceanographer, inventor, explorer, environmentalist, filmmaker, and writer. Born in France in 1910, Cousteau served in the French military during World War II. During that time, he met several men who enjoyed underwater exploration as much as he did. They worked together to build equipment that would help them see better underwater and stay under the water longer. They used common objects such as inner tubes and garden hoses to build masks and breathing devices. They also experimented with mechanical breathing devices such as oxygen tanks. Cousteau and his friends called the breathing device they built an aqualung. Today, we call it SCUBA (Self Contained Underwater Breathing Apparatus).

With the help of the aqualung, Cousteau was able to explore more places beneath the sea. He wanted to tell others about the beautiful fish and plants he saw so he took a waterproof camera with him when he dove.

Cousteau used his fame to help educate people about environmental issues such as ocean pollution and overpopulation. Cousteau received the Medal of Freedom from President Ronald Reagan in 1985. He continued to educate the public about protecting the environment until his death in 1997.

Sources: Cousteau Society, LibraryPoint.org, Eco-Photo Explorers

study pollution problems and possible chemical causes for plant and animal diseases in a particular region of the water. Geochemical oceanographers are called in after oil spills to check the level of damage to the water.

About 18 percent of oceanographers work for federal or state governments. Federal employers of oceanographers include the Environmental Protection Agency, the Department of Defense, and the Biological Resources Discipline of the U.S. Geological Survey, among others. State governments often employ oceanographers in environmental agencies or state-funded research projects. Forty percent of oceanographers work for colleges or universities as teachers and researchers. The remaining oceanographers work for private industries such as nonprofit organizations, oil and gas extraction companies, and industrial firms.

Education and Training

Science courses, including geology, biology, and chemistry, and math classes, such as algebra, trigonometry, and statistics, are especially important to take in high school. Because your work will involve a great deal of research and documentation, take English classes to improve your research and communication skills. In addition, take computer science classes because you will use computers throughout your professional life.

To become an oceanographer, you will need at least a bachelor's degree in chemistry, biology, geology, or physics. For most research or teaching positions, you will need a master's degree or doctoral degree in oceanography.

Earnings

According to the National Association of Colleges and Employers, students graduating with a bachelor's degree in geology and related sciences were offered an average starting salary of $40,786 in 2007. Salaries for geoscientists (a category that includes the career of oceanographer) ranged from less than $41,020 to more than $144,450, with a median of $75,800, according to the U.S. Department

Tips for Success

To be a successful oceanographer, you should

- have a strong interest in science, especially the physical and earth sciences
- have a curious nature
- enjoy being outdoors
- enjoy observing nature and performing experiments
- like reading, researching, and writing
- have good communication skills
- work well with others

FOR MORE INFO

For information on careers, education, and publications, contact
American Society of Limnology and Oceanography
5400 Bosque Boulevard, Suite 680
Waco, TX 76710-4446
800-929-2756
http://www.aslo.org

For information on how to join the MTS Club (for students from grades 6 to 12), contact

Marine Technology Society (MTS)
5565 Sterrett Place, Suite 108
Columbia, MD 21044-2606
410-884-5330
http://www.mtsociety.org

For ocean news, contact
The Oceanography Society
PO Box 1931
Rockville, MD 20849-1931
301-251-7708
info@tos.org
http://www.tos.org

of Labor. The average salary for experienced oceanographers working for the federal government was $88,820.

Outlook

Employment for all geoscientists (including oceanographers) is expected to be good. It is important to remember, though, that the job outlook for oceanographers can change according to the world market situation. The state of the offshore oil market, for instance, can affect the demand for geophysical oceanographers. Although the field of marine science is growing, researchers specializing in the popular field of biological oceanography, or marine biology, will face competition for available positions and research funding. However, the growing interest in understanding and protecting the environment will help to create new jobs. There will be more opportunities for oceanographers who study global climate change and fisheries science, as well as conduct marine biomedical and pharmaceutical research. Oceanographers who can speak a foreign language and who don't mind working outside the United States will have good job prospects.

Park Rangers

What Park Rangers Do

Park rangers protect animals and preserve forests, ponds, and other natural resources. They teach visitors about parks by giving lectures and tours. They also make sure rules and regulations are followed to maintain a safe environment for visitors and wildlife. For example, they make sure that visitors stay on trails away from dangerous geysers or hot springs or police the park to ensure that people are not driving motorized vehicles in areas where their presence could damage plants or wildlife. The National Park Service is one of the major employers of park

EXPLORING

- Read as much as you can about local, state, and national parks. The National Park Service's Web site, http://www.nps.gov, is a great place to start.
- If you are between the ages of five and 12, you can become a junior ranger at a National Park near you. Visit http://www.nps.gov/learn for details. If there isn't a participating park in your area, you can still get involved by becoming a Web ranger. Visit http://www.nps.gov/webrangers for more information.
- Get to know your local wildlife. What kind of insects, birds, fish, and other animals live in your area? Your science teacher or librarian will be able to help you find books that identify local flora and fauna.

Tips for Success

To be a successful park ranger, you should

- know how to protect plants and animals
- be a good teacher
- enjoy working outdoors
- have a pleasant personality
- be able to work with many different kinds of people
- be in good physical shape
- be able to enforce park rules and regulations
- be willing to travel to take on new assignments

rangers. In addition, park rangers work for other federal land and resource management agencies and similar state and local agencies.

Safety is a key responsibility for park rangers. They often require visitors to register at park offices so they will know when the visitors are expected to return from a hike or other activity. Rangers know first aid and, if there is an accident, they may have to help visitors who have been hurt. Rangers carefully mark hiking trails and other areas to reduce the risk of injuries for visitors and to protect plants and animals.

Rangers help visitors enjoy and learn about parks. They give lectures and provide guided tours of the park, explaining why certain plants and animals live there. They explain about the rocks and soil in the area and point out important historical sites.

Research and conservation efforts are also a big part of a park ranger's responsibilities. They study wildlife behavior by tagging and following certain animals. (Tagging involves placing an electronic collar or tracking device on an animal.) They may investigate sources of pollution that come from outside the park. Then they develop plans to help reduce pollution to make the park a better place for plants, animals, and visitors.

Rangers also do bookkeeping and other paperwork. They issue permits to visitors and keep track of how many people use the park. They also plan recreational activities and decide how to spend the money budgeted to the park.

Education and Training

In high school, take courses in earth science, biology, mathematics, history, English, and speech. Any classes or activities that deal with plant and animal life, the weather, geography, and interacting with others will be helpful.

Park rangers usually have bachelor's degrees in natural resource or recreational resource management. A degree in many other fields, such as biology or ecology, is also acceptable. Classes in forestry, geology, outdoor management, history, geography, behavioral sciences, and botany are helpful. Without a degree, you need at least three years of experience working in parks or conservation. Rangers also receive on-the-job training.

Earnings

In 2007, new rangers in the National Park Service earned between $27,026 and $35,135 annually. Rangers with some experience earned between $33,477 and $43,521. The most experienced rangers who supervise other workers earn more

Our National Parks

The National Park System in the United States was begun by Congress in 1872 when Yellowstone National Park was created. The National Park Service (NPS) is a bureau of the U.S. Department of the Interior. The NPS was created in 1916 to preserve, protect, and manage the national, cultural, historical, and recreational areas of the National Park System. At that time, the entire park system was less than one million acres. Today, the country's national parks cover more than 84 million acres of mountains, plains, deserts, swamps, historic sites, lakeshores, forests, rivers, battlefields, memorials, archaeological properties, and recreation areas.

A park ranger talks to visitors at Olympic National Park in Washington State. (David Frazier, The Image Works)

than $90,000 a year. The government may provide housing to rangers who work in remote areas.

Rangers in state parks work for the state government. Rangers employed by state parks earn average starting salaries of about $25,000.

Outlook

Many people want to become park rangers. In fact, there are not enough jobs for everyone who wants to enter the field. Park ranger jobs should continue to be popular in the future. Because of this stiff competition for positions, the job outlook is expected to change little. As a result, those interested in the field should attain the greatest number and widest variety of skills possible. They may wish to study subjects they can use in other fields, such as forestry, land management, conservation, wildlife management, history, and natural sciences.

Employment opportunities will be better at state and local parks—although these parks pay lower salaries than those offered by the National Park Service. Many park rangers start out as seasonal or part-time employees. This gives them a chance to break into the field and show their employers that they are good workers. In time, many part-time park rangers can transition to full-time positions. Aspiring park rangers must be willing to

FOR MORE INFO

For information about state parks and employment opportunities, contact
National Association of State Park Directors
8829 Woodyhill Road
Raleigh, NC 27613-1134
919-676-8365
NASPD@nc.rr.com
http://www.naspd.org

For general career information, contact the following organizations:
National Parks Conservation Association
1300 19th Street, NW, Suite 300
Washington, DC 20036-1628
800-628-7275
npca@npca.org
http://www.npca.org

National Recreation and Park Association
22377 Belmont Ridge Road
Ashburn, VA 20148-4150
800-626-6772

info@nrpa.org
http://www.nrpa.org

For detailed information about careers with the National Park Service, contact
National Park Service
U.S. Department of the Interior
1849 C Street, NW
Washington, DC 20240-0001
202-208-6843
http://www.nps.gov

Contact this organization for information on volunteer positions in natural resource management for high school students.
Student Conservation Association
689 River Road
PO Box 550
Charlestown, NH 03603-0550
603-543-1700
ask-us@thesca.org
http://www.thesca.org

travel to find jobs in the field. A position as a ranger with the National Park Service may not be available in one's own state or region, but at a park that is located across the country. The same is true for positions at the state level.

Range Managers

What Range Managers Do

Range managers help protect the environment. They improve and increase the food supply on rangeland, which covers more than one billion acres of land in the western United States and in Alaska. Range managers also may be called *range scientists, range ecologists,* and *range conservationists.*

Ranges are the source of food for both livestock and wildlife, but overgrazing by animals can leave the land bare. When there is neither grass nor shrubs on open land, soil erosion occurs. Range managers are in charge of erosion-control programs, such as irrigation and rotating grazing lands.

Range managers make sure the land provides as rich a source of food as possible. They study rangelands to decide the number and kinds of cattle that can best graze on these lands and the times of year that are best for grazing. They also study different varieties of plants. They do this to determine which ones will grow best and which might actually be harmful to the land and its wildlife.

Range managers try to conserve, or protect, the land for a variety of other uses, such as outdoor recreation, timber, and habitats for many kinds of wildlife. They look for ways to prevent damage by fire and rodents. If a fire does occur, range managers try to restore the land. They make sure fences and corrals are in good condition, and water reservoirs (storage areas) are well maintained.

Most range managers work in the western part of the United States or in Alaska, where most of the nation's rangelands are located.

In addition to scientific skills, range managers must be able to speak and write effectively. They should also be able to work well with others. They should have a love for the outdoors and be willing to work in all types of weather—from rain or snow to extreme heat. Finally, range managers should be in good health and have physical stamina for the strenuous activity that this job requires.

DID YOU KNOW?

Where Range Managers Work

- Federal government agencies such as the Forest Service, Natural Resources Conservation Service, Bureau of Indian Affairs, and Bureau of Land Management
- State government organizations such as game and fish departments, state land agencies, and extension services
- Oil and coal companies
- Colleges and universities
- Banks and real estate firms

Education and Training

To prepare for a career as a range manager, take classes in biology, chemistry, physics, and mathematics. Business classes also will be helpful for learning aspects of management. Range managers must have a bachelor's degree in range science, soil science, or natural resource management. Typical classes for range science students include Rangeland Ecology and Management, Range Ecology-Grasslands, Range Ecology-

What Is Rangeland?

According to the Idaho Rangeland Resource Division, rangeland can be defined as land that is "not farmed, that is not forested, and that is not covered by glaciers, solid rock, concrete, or asphalt." Many types of ecosystems are found on rangelands including grasslands, deserts, prairies, marshes, savannas, tundra, and open woodland. More than 40 percent of the earth is covered by rangeland.

Shrublands, Wildland Plant Identification, Desert Watershed Management, Wildland Restoration and Ecology, Rangeland Analysis, Rangeland-Animal Relations, Rangeland Management Planning, Principles of Soil Science, Natural Resource Economics and Policy, Introduction to Statistical Methods, and Technical Writing. For many range manager positions you need a graduate degree in one of these fields.

Earnings

According to the U.S. Department of Labor, beginning range managers with bachelor's degrees working for the federal government earned $28,862 to $35,752 in 2006. Those with master's degrees earned $43,731 to $52,912, and those with doctorates started at $63,417 or more. The average federal salary for rangeland managers was $60,828 in 2007. State governments and private companies pay their range managers salaries that are about the same as those paid by the federal government.

Outlook

Employment for range managers is expected to be slow in coming years. This is a small career field, and most of the

FOR MORE INFO

For information on careers, colleges that offer range management education, and membership for high school students, contact
Society for Range Management
10030 West 27th Avenue
Wheat Ridge, CO 80215-6601
303-986-3309
info@rangelands.org
http://www.rangelands.org

For information about career opportunities with the federal government, contact
Bureau of Land Management
U.S. Department of the Interior
1849 C Street

Washington, DC 20240-0001
http://www.blm.gov

Natural Resources Conservation Service
U.S. Department of Agriculture
1400 Independence Avenue, SW
Washington, DC 20250-0002
http://www.nrcs.usda.gov

U.S. Forest Service
U.S. Department of Agriculture
1400 Independence Avenue, SW
Washington, DC 20250-0003
800-832-1355
http://www.fs.fed.us

openings will arise when older, experienced range managers retire or leave the occupation for other reasons. Range managers will still be needed to help develop and manage rangeland. They will also be hired to change rangeland to land that can be used for wildlife habitat and public recreation. Range specialists will also find jobs in private industry, reclaiming lands damaged by oil and coal exploration.

Soil Conservationists and Technicians

What Soil Conservationists and Technicians Do

Soil is all around us. It is in parks and farm fields and at the bottom of streams and in your backyard. If there was no soil, trees and plants would not be able to grow. They also might blow away in the wind. For this reason, it is important to protect soil and

EXPLORING

- Join a chapter of the National 4-H Council (http://www.fourh-council.edu) or National FFA Organization (http://www.ffa.org).
- Visit the following Web sites to learn more about soil and soil conservation: Dig It: The Secrets of Soil (http://forces.si.edu/soils), The Field Museum Underground Adventure (http://www.fieldmuseum.org/undergroun-dadventure), and Just for Kids:

Soil Biological Communities (http://www.blm.gov/nstc/soil/Kids).
- Science courses that include lab sections and mathematics courses that focus on practical problem solving will also help give you a feel for this kind of work.
- Ask your teacher or guidance counselor to arrange an interview with a soil conservationist or technician.

DID YOU KNOW?

Where Soil Conservationists and Technicians Work

- Federal government agencies such as the Natural Resources Conservation Service, the Bureau of Land Management, and the Bureau of Reclamation
- State and county soil conservation agencies
- Mining companies
- Public utilities companies
- Self-employment

use it wisely. *Soil conservationists* and *soil conservation technicians* are workers who protect the soil.

Soil conservationists develop conservation plans to help farmers and ranchers, developers, homeowners, and government officials use their land in the best way while still following government conservation regulations. They suggest plans to conserve and reclaim soil and preserve or restore wetlands and other rare ecological areas. They also give advice on rotating crops for increased yields (or harvests) and soil conservation, reducing water pollution, and restoring or increasing wildlife populations. They assess the land users' needs, costs, maintenance requirements, and the life expectancy of various conservation practices. Soil conservationists also give talks to various organizations to teach land users and the public in general how to conserve and restore soil and water resources. Much of their advice is based on information provided to them by *soil scientists,* who are experts in the study of soil.

Soil conservation technicians work more directly with land users by putting the ideas and plans of the conservationist into action. They take soil samples. They help landowners select, install, and maintain measures that conserve and improve soil, plant, water, marsh, wildlife, and recreational resources.

When a soil conservationist designs a new conservation plan for a landowner, technicians inspect the different phases of the project as it is constructed. They might inspect ponds, structures, dams, tile, outlet terraces, and animal waste control facilities.

Soil conservation technicians mainly work with farmers and agricultural issues. They also work with land developers and local governments to prevent soil erosion and preserve wetlands. Erosion is the wearing away of soil and other land features by water, wind, and human activities, such as farming and construction.

Soil conservationists and technicians must be very knowledgeable about soil and water science. They should enjoy working outdoors in all types of weather and be in good physical shape in order to walk to locations that are sometimes remote. Soil conservationists and technicians should be able to write easy-to-understand reports that detail their tests, studies, and recommendations. Good oral communication skills also are important.

Education and Training

To prepare for a career as a soil conservationist, be sure to take as many science classes as possible, including earth science, biology, and chemistry. If your high school offers agriculture classes, take any relating to land use, crop production, and soils. Also take math classes such as algebra, geometry, and trigonometry. Take several years of English to develop your writing, research, and speaking skills. You will need these skills when writing reports and working with others.

Soil conservationists have bachelor's degrees in areas such as general agriculture, range management, crop or soil science, forestry, and agricultural engineering. If you want to teach or work in a research position, you will need

Get Started!

Here are seven things you can do to help improve the soil:

1. Start a compost pile
2. Start a worm compost pile
3. Recycle yard waste
4. Support organic farmers
5. Plant a garden
6. Plant native species
7. Clean up a polluted park, riverbank, or other area

Source: The Field Museum

FOR MORE INFO

Contact the NRCS for information on government soil conservation careers. Its Web site has information on becoming an Earth Team volunteer.
Natural Resources Conservation Service (NRCS)
U.S. Department of Agriculture
1400 Independence Avenue, SW
Washington, DC 20250-0002
http://www.nrcs.usda.gov

For information on educational institutions offering soil science programs, contact
National Society of Consulting Soil Scientists
PO Box 1724
Sandpoint, ID 83864-0901

800-535-7148
http://www.nscss.org

For information on soil conservation and publications, contact
Soil and Water Conservation Society
7515 Ankeny Road, NE
Ankeny, IA 50023-9723
515-289-2331
http://www.swcs.org

To read *Soils Sustain Life*, visit the society's Web site.
Soil Science Society of America
677 South Segoe Road
Madison, WI 53711-1086
608-273-8080
http://www.soils.org

a master's degree in a natural resources field. Government jobs do not necessarily require a college degree. A combination of experience in the field and education can serve as substitute. But a college education will give you a better chance of landing a job.

Soil conservation technicians need at least a high school diploma. Courses in math, speech, writing, chemistry, and biology are important. Courses in vocational agriculture, which is the study of farming as an occupation, also are helpful.

Some technical institutes and junior or community colleges offer associate's degrees in soil conservation. First-year courses in these programs include basic soils, chemistry, botany, zoology, and range management. Second-year courses include surveying, forestry, game management, fish management, and soil and water conservation.

Earnings

The U.S. Department of Labor reports that median earnings for soil and plant scientists were $58,000 in 2007. Scientists who were new to the field earned less than $34,620. Those with a lot of experience earned $100,800 or more annually. Soil and plant scientists who worked for the federal government earned average salaries of about $75,000 in 2008. Those employed by colleges and universities earned about $51,000. The U.S. Department of Labor reports that average earnings for forest and conservation technicians (including those who specialize in soil science) were $33,520 in 2007. Salaries ranged from less than $23,460 to more than $51,040 annually.

Outlook

Employment within the field of soil conservation is expected to grow more slowly than the average for all careers. Despite this prediction, many jobs should be available with the federal government and with private consulting companies. Most soil conservationists and technicians work for the federal government, so job opportunities will depend in large part on government spending. If the government spends a lot of money on soil conservation, there will be many job openings. If the government cuts the money it spends, there will be fewer jobs.

Most of America's cropland has suffered from some sort of erosion, so soil conservation professionals will be needed to help prevent a dangerous depletion of fertile soil.

Soil Scientists

What Soil Scientists Do

Soil is one of our most important natural resources. It provides the nutrients necessary to grow food for billions of people. To use soil wisely and keep it from washing away or being damaged, experts must analyze, or study, it and find the best ways to manage it. *Soil scientists* are these experts. Soil scientists collect soil samples and study their chemical and physical characteristics. They study how soil responds to fertilizers and other farming practices. This helps farmers decide what types of crops to grow on certain soils.

EXPLORING

- Visit the following Web sites to learn more about soil and soil conservation: Dig It: The Secrets of Soil (http://forces.si.edu/soils), The Field Museum Underground Adventure (http://www.fieldmuseum.org/undergroundadventure), and Just for Kids: Soil Biological Communities (http://www.blm.gov/nstc/soil/Kids).

- Join a chapter of the National 4-H Council (http://www.fourhcouncil.edu) or National FFA Organization (http://www.ffa.org).

- If you live in an agricultural community, look for part-time or summer work on a farm or ranch.

Words to Learn

aeration porosity The fraction of the volume of soil that is filled with air at any given time.

blowout A small area from which soil material has been removed by wind.

creep Slow mass movement of soil and soil material down steep slopes. Creep is primarily caused by gravity, but aided by saturation with water and by alternate freezing and thawing.

dunes Wind-built ridges and hills of sand formed in the same manner as snowdrifts.

erosion The wearing away of soil and other land features by water, wind, and human activities, such as farming and construction.

fertilizer Natural and chemical elements that help plants to grow. Chemical fertilizers can be harmful if used in too large quantities.

gytta Peat consisting of plant and animal remains from standing water.

karst Topography with caves, sinkholes, and underground drainage that is formed in limestone and other rocks by dissolution.

macronutrient A nutrient found in high amounts in a plant.

nutrient A substance that encourages growth.

scarp A cliff or steep slope along the edge of a plateau.

Soil scientists often work outdoors. They go to fields to take soil samples. They spend many hours meeting with farmers and discussing ways to avoid soil damage. They may suggest that a farmer grow crops on different parts of a farm every few years so that the unused soil can recover. Soil scientists may also recommend that a farmer use various fertilizers to put nutrients back into the soil. They may suggest ways to protect the crops to keep the wind from blowing the soil away.

Soil scientists work for agricultural research laboratories, crop production companies, and other organizations. They also work with road departments to advise them about the quality and condition of the soil over which roads will be built.

Some soil scientists travel to foreign countries to conduct research and learn how other scientists treat the soil. Many also teach at colleges, universities, and agricultural schools.

Soil scientists must be able to work on their own and with other scientists and technicians. They must be willing to spend many hours outdoors in all kinds of weather. Soil scientists should be detail-oriented in order to do accurate research, and they should enjoy solving problems. For example, they should like trying to figure out why a crop isn't flourishing and what fertilizers should be used or develop ways to protect crops from erosion. Soil scientists should be organized, effective time managers, and be comfortable using technology such as computers. They should not mind getting dirty while conducting research in the field.

The Dirt on Soil

Soil is a combination of plant, animal, mineral, and other matter. It contains sand, silt, and clay particles, as well as water, air, and many different microorganisms.

Soil provides all but three of the 16 nutrients that plants need to grow. Soil also releases these nutrients into streams and oceans, where it helps fish and other water life.

Soil cleans water. Nearly all fresh water travels over soil or through soil before it enters rivers, lakes, and aquifers. The processes that take place in the upper layers of soil help remove many impurities from the water and kill some disease-causing organisms. Soil helps prevent flooding by soaking up large amounts of rain and distributing it to water bodies over days, months, or years.

Source: Soil and Water
Conservation Society

FOR MORE INFO

Contact the NRCS for information on government soil conservation careers. Its Web site has information on becoming an Earth Team volunteer.
Natural Resources Conservation Service (NRCS)
U.S. Department of Agriculture
1400 Independence Avenue, SW
Washington, DC 20250-0002
http://www.nrcs.usda.gov

For information on educational institutions offering soil science programs, contact
National Society of Consulting Soil Scientists
PO Box 1724
Sandpoint, ID 83864-0901

800-535-7148
http://www.nscss.org

For information on soil conservation and publications, contact
Soil and Water Conservation Society
7515 Ankeny Road, NE
Ankeny, IA 50023-9723
515-289-2331
http://www.swcs.org

To read *Soils Sustain Life,* visit the society's Web site.
Soil Science Society of America
677 South Segoe Road
Madison, WI 53711-1086
608-273-8080
http://www.soils.org

Education and Training

To be a soil scientist, you need a solid background in mathematics and science, especially the physical and earth sciences.

The best way to become a soil scientist is to go to college and earn a bachelor's degree. Then you should go on to earn a master's degree in agricultural or soil science. Typical classes for soil science majors include Statistics, Mathematics, General Soils, Soil Morphology/Classification/Mapping, Soil Physics, Soil Chemistry, Soil Biology, Soil Fertility, and Technical Writing. A degree in biology, physics, or chemistry might also be acceptable, but you should take some courses in agriculture. With a bachelor's degree in agricultural science, you can get some nonresearch jobs, but you will not be able to advance very far. Most research and teaching positions require a doctorate.

Earnings

According to the U.S. Department of Labor, average earnings for soil and plant scientists were $58,000 in 2007. Workers who were just starting out in the field made $34,000 or less. Soil and plant scientists with a lot of experience earned more than $100,800. Salaries for soil scientists who work for the federal government are higher. In 2007, they had average earnings of $72,800 a year.

Outlook

Agricultural problems will continue to be an issue in the United States in the coming years. Soil scientists should find plenty of job opportunities. There have not been as many agricultural students in the past few years as there were in the past. This will create more job openings.

Soil scientists will be able to find jobs with private companies, such as seed, fertilizer, and farm equipment companies, as well as with government agencies. There will be more opportunities in teaching and in research.

Tree Experts

What Tree Experts Do

Trees and shrubs need more than just sunlight and water to live. They also need regular care, occasional diagnosis, and treatment. *Tree experts* practice arboriculture, which is the

EXPLORING

- Visit http://www.treesaregood. org to learn more about the benefits of trees.
- Plant a tree in your background or neighborhood. Visit the following Web sites to learn how to plant a tree: American Forests: How to Plant a Tree (http://www.americanforests. org/planttrees/howto.php), How to Plant a Tree (http://www. ehow.com/how_2379114_plant- tree.html), TreeHelp.com: How to Plant a Tree (http://www. treehelp.com/howto/howto- plant-a-tree.asp).

- Look up the types of trees in a tree identification guide. Try to name ones that are in your neighborhood. Here are some tree resources to explore: *The Illustrated Encyclopedia of Trees of the World,* by Catherine Cutler, Tony Russell, and Martin Walters (Lorenz Books, 2007); *National Geographic Field Guide to Trees of North America,* by Keith Rush- forth and Charles Hollis (National Geographic, 2006); and *Trees: A Visual Guide,* by Tony Rodd and Jennifer Stackhouse (University of California Press, 2008).

DID YOU KNOW?

- An acre of trees absorbs the same amount of carbon that is produced by a car that has been driven up to 8,700 miles.
- Trees act as sound barriers and reduce noise.
- Trees planted near homes reduce heating and cooling costs. They also increase the value of your home by 25 percent.
- Trees improve water and air quality.

Sources: International Society of Arboriculture, Tree Care Industry Association

care of trees and shrubs, especially those in urban areas (cities and towns). They are sometimes called *arborists*.

Tree experts prune, or cut, trees to control their shape. They trim branches if they interfere with power lines, cross property lines, or grow too close to buildings. Tree experts use pruning shears or hand and power saws to do the cutting. If the branches are large or wide, tree experts may rope them together before they begin to saw. After they are cut, the branches can be safely lowered to the ground. Tree experts use ladders, aerial lifts, and cranes to reach extremely tall trees. Sometimes, cables or braces are used on tree limbs weakened by disease or old age, or damaged by a storm.

When cities or towns plan a new development, they ask tree experts to recommend what types of trees to plant. Tree experts suggest the best trees for a particular environment.

A large part of keeping a tree healthy is the prevention of disease. There are a number of diseases, insects, bacteria, fungi, viruses, and other organisms that can hurt, or even kill, trees. Tree experts are trained to diagnose the problem and suggest the proper remedy. For example, they might recommend chemical insecticides or the use of natural insect predators to combat an insect problem.

Trees, especially young plantings, often need extra nourishment, or food. Tree experts are trained to apply fertilizers, both natural and chemical, in a safe and environmentally friendly manner. They are also hired by golf courses and parks to install lightning protection systems for trees.

Tree experts, of course, should not be afraid of heights. They climb trees that are more than 50 feet tall to do their work. They

An arborist measures a hemlock tree in the Great Smoky Mountains National Park. (Joe Howell, Knoxville News-Sentinel/AP Images)

rely on cleated shoes, security belts, and safety hoists to keep them safe. Tree experts need to be in excellent physical shape because their job is very physically demanding. They should enjoy working outdoors. Finally, they should be willing to continue to learn about tree science and developments in the field throughout their careers.

Education and Training

Biology classes can provide a solid background for a career in arboriculture. An interest in gardening, conservation, and the outdoors is also helpful. Entry-level workers such as assistants or climbers do not need to have advanced education. If you plan to make this field your career, a college education will help you obtain advanced positions and earn a higher salary. Several colleges and universities offer arboriculture and related programs, such as landscape design, nursery stock production, or grounds and turf maintenance.

On-the-job training lasting about one to three months is available for some positions. Trainees get their start by loading and unloading the equipment, gathering debris, and helping other workers. In time, trainees are allowed to operate small pieces of equipment. After sufficient experience, workers are allowed to climb trees and operate larger pieces of machinery.

Earnings

Entry-level positions, such as grounds workers or trainees, pay between $7 and $10 an hour. Supervisors with three or more years of experience earn from $20 to $30 an hour. Private consultants with eight to 10 years of experience or arborists in sales positions can earn $50,000 to $60,000 or more annually. Arborists who work in busy urban areas tend to earn more.

Outlook

The outlook for tree experts is good. People are becoming more interested in the environment. They find that trees and shrubs make their neighborhoods nicer places to live. Arborists will be needed to keep these trees and shrubs healthy, and make sure that trees do not interfere with power lines and buildings. They will also be in demand to protect forests from invasive species. An invasive species is a type of organism that does not typically live in an area and that has been brought in accidentally via

FOR MORE INFO

To learn more about career paths in arboriculture, visit the society's Web site.
International Society of Arboriculture
PO Box 3129
Champaign, IL 61826-3129
888-472-8733
isa@isa-arbor.com
http://www.isa-arbor.com

For information on urban forestry, contact
Society of Municipal Arborists
http://www.urban-forestry.com

For information on careers in arboriculture, contact
Tree Care Industry Association
136 Harvey Road, Suite 101
Londonderry, NH 03053-7439
800-733-2622
http://www.treecareindustry.org

truck, ship, or another method. An example of an invasive species is the Asian long-horn beetle. The beetles were unknowingly transported to the United States via packing material. By the time the insects were discovered, the beetles had damaged hundreds of mature trees throughout New York, Chicago, and surrounding areas. Thousands of trees had to be cut down. Arborists, especially those trained to diagnose and treat such cases, will be in demand to work in urban areas.

Wildlife Photographers

What Wildlife Photographers Do

Wildlife photographers take photographs and make films of animals in their natural environment. The photographs are used in science publications, research reports, textbooks, newspapers, magazines, and many other printed materials. Films are used in research and for professional and public education. Photographs and films are also used on Web sites and in e-books and e-magazines.

Wildlife photographers often find themselves in swamps, deserts, jungles, at the tops of trees or in underground tunnels, swim-

EXPLORING

- Take classes in photography, media arts (film, sound recording), and life sciences.
- Join photography clubs or enter contests that encourage you to use camera equipment.
- Learn how to use different types of film, lenses, and filters.
- Learn how to use a digital camera.

- Practice taking pictures of birds and other animals at parks, nature centers, and zoos.
- Watch nature shows and videos to learn more about both animal behavior and filming animals in the wild.
- Read books and magazines about animals—especially those that feature photographs of animals in their native habitat.

ming in the ocean or hanging from the side of a mountain. They may shoot pictures of the tiniest insects (such as the red headed ash borer) or the largest mammals (such as the blue whale).

Some wildlife photographers focus on one family or species or in one region or area. For example, some wildlife photographers may shoot chimpanzees in their various habitats in Africa—from humid forests to savanna-woodlands. Another photographer might shoot various species of birds that live in the southwestern United States, such as the roadrunner and elf owl.

Like other professional photographers, wildlife photographers must know about light, camera settings, lenses, film, filters, and digital photography. In addition, they must be able to take pictures without disturbing the animals or natural settings that they photograph. To do this, they must learn about the animals and plants they use as subjects before they go into the wild. For example, they must know how close they can get to a buffalo before it might get mad and charge them and what plants, such as poison ivy, might cause them discomfort if touched.

All photographers should have manual dexterity, good eyesight and color vision, and artistic ability. They should be patient since it may take hours or even days to take just the right photograph. Self-employed (or freelance) photographers need good business skills. They must be able to manage their own studios, including hiring and managing assistants and other employees, keeping records, and maintaining photographic and business files. Marketing and sales skills are also important for successful freelance photographers.

Wildlife photographers do not necessarily need to be zoologists, although a background in biology or zoology is helpful for this career. After many years of experience, wildlife photographers often become experts in the behavior of the animals they photograph. It is also possible for zoologists who use photography in their research to eventually become expert wildlife photographers.

A wildlife photographer prepares for a shot. (Eastcott-Momatiuk, The Image Works)

The technological advances in photography and the expertise of wildlife photographers have contributed much to scientific knowledge about animal behavior, new species, evolution, and animals' roles in preserving or changing the environment.

Wildlife photographers are employed by publishing companies, television stations (such as Animal Planet), nonprofit agencies, government agencies (such as the National Park Service), and any other organization that requires photographs or videos of wildlife and nature. Some wildlife photographers are employed as teachers at colleges and universities, while still operating a freelance business in their spare time.

Education and Training

There are no formal education requirements for becoming a wildlife photographer. A high school diploma is recommended for this career. Earning a college degree will help you learn

Fame and Fortune: Ansel Adams (1902–84)

Ansel Adams was one of the most famous nature photographers in the world. He is best known for his beautiful images of the American West and for his contributions to photographic technology.

Adams was born in San Francisco, California. In 1916, he convinced his parents to go to Yosemite National Park. They gave him his first camera—a Kodak Box Brownie—and his love of photography began. In 1919, he joined the Sierra Club, an environmental conservation organization. The next year, he had his first photograph published in the organization's magazine.

During this time, Adams studied music and photography and set a goal of becoming a concert pianist for his career. But by the late 1920s, Adams realized that his true love was photography. In the following decades, he became well-known for his nature photographs—many of natural areas in Yosemite. He published many photography books, was honored with solo exhibitions, and cofounded the photography department at the Museum of Modern Art (1940). He also was an active conservationist and supporter of social justice issues. During World War II, he even went to Manzanar (http://www.nps.gov/manz), an internment camp in California, to take photographs of imprisoned Japanese Americans in order to educate the public about this injustice. Adams also served on the board of directors of the Sierra Club from 1934 to 1971 and also became active in The Wilderness Society.

In 1980, President Jimmy Carter presented Adams with the Presidential Medal of Freedom, the highest honor awarded to civilians. After his death, Congress passed a law that designated more than 200,000 acres near Yosemite as the Ansel Adams Wilderness Area (http://sierranevadawild.gov/wild/ansel-adams).

Visit http://www.pbs.org/wgbh/amex/ansel for more information on this groundbreaking photographer.

On the Web

Visit the following Web sites to learn how to photograph wildlife and natural areas:

HOW TO PHOTOGRAPH WILDLIFE LIKE A PRO
http://www.travellady.com/Issues/November08/5359photograph.htm

PHOTOGRAPHY BASICS
http://www.photography-basics.com/page/4

WILDLIFE RESEARCH PHOTOGRAPHY
http://www.moosepeterson.com/home.html

about both photography and biology. A bachelor of arts in photography or film with a minor in biology would prepare you well for a career as a wildlife photographer. While in school, you should try to gain practical experience and build a portfolio of your work. A portfolio is a collection of your best work.

Wildlife photographers must not risk the well-being of any animal to take a picture. They must show concern for the environment in their work. They must use common sense and not anger or frighten any animals while trying to take a picture.

Earnings

Full-time wildlife photographers earn salaries that range from about $19,000 to $41,000 a year. Most wildlife photographers work as freelancers. Wildlife photographers who combine scientific training and photographic expertise usually start at higher salaries than other photographers. It can be hard to earn a living as a wildlife photographer, so you may have to

FOR MORE INFO

For information on nature photography, contact
North American Nature Photography Association
10200 West 44th Avenue, Suite 304
Wheat Ridge, CO 80033-2840
303-422-8527
info@nanpa.org
http://www.nanpa.org

For information on photography careers, contact
Professional Photographers of America
229 Peachtree Street, NE, Suite 2200
Atlanta, GA 30303-1608
800-786-6277
http://www.ppa.com

earn additional money by working in another occupation or do other kinds of photography until you become known for your work as a wildlife photographer.

Outlook

Employment of photographers in all fields is expected to be steady. The demand for new photographs and videos of animals in their natural habitats should remain strong. Researchers, book and magazine editors, and television stations all need photographs and videos of wildlife. It is important to remember that only a few people work as full-time wildlife photographers. People who know a lot about nature and digital photography will have the best job prospects.

Zoologists

What Zoologists Do

Zoologists are biologists who study animals. They usually specialize in one animal group. *Entomologists* are experts on insects. *Ornithologists* study birds. *Mammalogists* focus on mammals. *Herpetologists* specialize in reptiles. *Ichthyologists* study fish. Some zoologists specialize even more and focus on a specific part or aspect of an animal. For example, a zoologist might study single-celled organisms, a particular variety of fish (such as the green back cutthroat trout), or the

EXPLORING

- Volunteer at your local zoo or aquarium.
- Ask your school librarian to help you find books and videos on animal behavior.
- Explore hobbies such as bird-watching, insect collecting, or raising hamsters, rabbits, and other pets.
- Offer to pet sit for your neighbors. This will give you a chance to observe and care for animals.
- Interview a zoologist about his or her career. Ask the following questions: What made you want to enter the field? What do you like most and least about your job? How did you train to become a zoologist? What advice would you give to someone who is interested in the career?

DID YOU KNOW?

- The world's largest dog on record was an Old English Mastiff, named Zorba. He weighed 343 pounds and was 8 feet 3 inches long from nose to tail.
- The smallest dog on record was a Yorkie from Blackburn, England, who was 2.5 inches tall and 3.75 inches long. He weighed only 4 ounces.
- The world's smallest cat on record was a male Blue Point Himalayan-Persian named Tinker Toy. He was 2.75 inches tall and 7.5 inches long.
- The cheetah is the fastest land animal. It is the only cat that can't retract its claws.
- The world's largest bird is the male African ostrich. They have been recorded to measure 9 feet tall and weigh 345 pounds.
- The world's smallest bird is the adult male bee hummingbird of Cuba. It is 2.24 inches long and weighs 0.056 ounces.

Source: Amazing Animal Facts

behavior of one group of animals, such as elephants, owls, or orangutans.

Some zoologists are primarily teachers. Others spend most of their time doing research. Nearly all zoologists spend a major portion of their time at the computer. Most zoologists spend very little time outdoors (an average of two to eight weeks per year). In fact, junior scientists often spend more time in the field than senior scientists do. Senior scientists coordinate research, supervise other workers, and try to find funding. Raising money is an extremely important activity for zoologists who work for government agencies or universities. They need the money to pay for research and fieldwork.

Basic research zoologists conduct experiments on live or dead animals, in a laboratory or in natural surroundings. They make discoveries that might help humans. Such research in the past has led to discoveries about nutrition, aging, food production, and pest control. Some research zoologists work in the field with

A zoologist studies a Rhea chick. (Kai-Uwe Knoth, AP Images)

wild animals, such as whales or wolves. They trace their movements with radio transmitters and observe their eating habits, mating patterns, and other behavior. Researchers use all kinds of laboratory chemicals and equipment such as dissecting tools, microscopes, slides, electron microscopes, and other complicated machinery.

Zoologists in applied research use basic research to solve problems in medicine, conservation, and aquarium and zoo work. For example, applied researchers may develop a new drug for people or animals. Others may invent a new pesticide or a new type of pet food. (A pesticide is a substance, often made from chemicals, that is used to stop a pest—an animal, insect, or other organism—from hurting plants or animals.)

Many zoologists teach in colleges and universities while they do their own research. Some zoologists manage zoos and aquariums. Still others work for government agencies, private businesses, and research organizations.

Successful zoologists have a strong love of science. They are willing to work long hours conducting research. Zoologists should be able to work on a variety of tasks at one time. For example, a typical workweek might involve conducting research in the field and in the laboratory, writing articles about their work, seeking out funding for projects, and explaining their findings to the public and other scientists. Zoologists should be organized and have excellent time management skills. Strong communication skills are also important.

Education and Training

Science classes, especially in biology, are important if you want to become a zoologist. You should also study English, communications, and computer science.

After high school, you must go to college to earn a bachelor's degree. A master's or doctoral degree is usually also required. You do not need to specialize until you enter a master's degree program.

Earnings

Zoologists earned average salaries of about $55,000 a year in 2007, according to the U.S. Department of Labor. Beginning salaries for those with a bachelor's degree in biological and life sciences

DID YOU KNOW?

Where Zoologists Work

- Zoos
- Aquariums
- Museums
- Colleges and universities
- Nonprofit organizations

FOR MORE INFO

For information about a career as a zoologist, contact

American Institute of Biological Sciences
1444 I Street, NW, Suite 200
Washington, DC 20005-6535
202-628-1500
http://www.aibs.org

For information about all areas of zoology, contact

Society for Integrative and Comparative Biology
1313 Dolly Madison Boulevard, Suite 402
McLean, VA 22101-3926
800-955-1236
http://www.sicb.org

were $34,953, according to the National Association of Colleges and Employers. Zoologists who work for the federal government earned average salaries of about $69,630.

Outlook

Employment for zoologists is expected to be good in the coming years. This is because there is more interest in protecting and studying animals. But since this field is small, there will be a lot of competition for research jobs. Zoologists with advanced degrees and years of research experience in their specialty will enjoy the best job prospects.

Glossary

accredited approved as meeting established standards for providing good training and education; this approval is usually given by an independent organization of professionals.

annual salary the money an individual earns for an entire year of work.

apprentice a person who is learning a trade by working under the supervision of a skilled worker; apprentices often receive classroom instruction in addition to their supervised practical experience

associate's degree an academic rank or title granted by a community or junior college or similar institution to graduates of a two-year program of education beyond high school

bachelor's degree an academic rank or title given to a person who has completed a four-year program of study at a college or university; also called an *undergraduate degree* or *baccalaureate*

career an occupation for which a worker receives training and has an opportunity for advancement

certified approved as meeting established requirements for skill, knowledge, and experience in a particular field; people are certified by the organization of professionals in their field

college a higher education institution that is above the high school level

community college a public or private two-year college attended by students who do not usually live at the college; graduates of a community college receive an associate's degree and may transfer to a four-year college or university to complete a bachelor's degree

diploma a certificate or document given by a school to show that a person has completed a course or has graduated from the school

distance education   a type of educational program that allows students to take classes and complete their education by mail or the Internet

doctorate   the highest academic rank or title granted by a graduate school to a person who has completed a two- to three-year program after having received a master's degree

freelancer   a worker who is not a regular employee of a company; they work for themselves and do not receive a regular paycheck

fringe benefit   a payment or benefit to an employee in addition to regular wages or salary; examples of fringe benefits include a pension, a paid vacation, and health or life insurance

graduate school   school that people may attend after they have received their bachelor's degree; people who complete an educational program at a graduate school earn a master's degree or a doctorate

intern   an advanced student (usually one with at least some college training) in a professional field who is employed in a job that is intended to provide supervised practical experience for the student

internship   the position or job of an intern

junior college   a two-year college that offers courses like those in the first half of a four-year college program; graduates of a junior college usually receive an associate's degree and may transfer to a four-year college or university to complete a bachelor's degree

liberal arts   the subjects covered by college courses that develop broad general knowledge rather than specific occupational skills; the liberal arts are often considered to include philosophy, literature and the arts, history, language, and some courses in the social sciences and natural sciences

major   the academic field in which a college student specializes and receives a degree

master's degree   an academic rank or title granted by a graduate school to a person who has completed a one- or two-year program after having received a bachelor's degree

pension   an amount of money paid regularly by an employer to a former employee after he or she retires from working

scholarship   a gift of money to a student to help the student pay for further education

social studies   courses of study (such as civics, geography, and history) that deal with how human societies work

starting salary   salary paid to a newly hired employee; the starting salary is usually a smaller amount than is paid to a more experienced worker

technical college   a private or public college offering two- or four-year programs in technical subjects; technical colleges offer courses in both general and technical subjects and award associate's degrees and bachelor's degrees

undergraduate   a student at a college or university who has not yet received a degree

undergraduate degree   *see* **bachelor's degree**

union   an organization whose members are workers in a particular industry or company; the union works to gain better wages, benefits, and working conditions for its members; also called a *labor union* or *trade union*

vocational school   a public or private school that offers training in one or more skills or trades

wage   money that is paid in return for work done, especially money paid on the basis of the number of hours or days worked

Browse and Learn More

Books

Anderson, Alan, Gwen Diehn, and Terry Krautwurst. *Geology Crafts For Kids: 50 Nifty Projects to Explore the Marvels of Planet Earth.* New York: Sterling Publishing Company, 1998.

Arthus-Bertrand, Yann. *The Future of the Earth: An Introduction to Sustainable Development for Young Readers.* New York: Harry N. Abrams, 2004.

Blobaum, Cindy. *Geology Rocks!: 50 Hands-On Activities to Explore the Earth.* Nashville, Tenn.: Williamson Publishing Company, 1999.

Challen, Paul C. *Environmental Disaster Alert!* New York: Crabtree Publishing Company, 2004.

Claybourne, Anna, Gillian Doherty, and Rebecca Treays. *Encyclopedia of Planet Earth.* Tulsa, Okla.: Usborne Publishing, 2000.

Cutler, Catherine, Tony Russell, and Martin Walters. *The Illustrated Encyclopedia of Trees of the World.* London, U.K.: Lorenz Books, 2007.

David, Laurie, and Cambria Gordon. *Down-to-Earth Guide to Global Warming.* New York: Scholastic, 2007.

Donald, Rhonda Lucas. *Air Pollution.* New York: Children's Press, 2002.

Donald, Rhonda Lucas. *Endangered Animals.* New York: Children's Press, 2002.

Donald, Rhonda Lucas. *Water Pollution.* New York: Children's Press, 2002.

Farndon, John. *The Illustrated Encyclopedia of Rocks of the World: A Practical Guide to Over 150 Igneous, Metamorphic and Sedimentary Rocks.* London, U.K.: Southwater, 2007.

Farndon, John. *Practical Encyclopedia of Rocks & Minerals.* London, U.K.: Lorenz Books, 2006.

Heitzmann, William Ray. *Opportunities in Marine Science and Maritime Careers.* New York: McGraw-Hill, 2006.

Kellert, Stephen, and Matthew Black. *The Encyclopedia of the Environment.* New York: Franklin Watts, 1999.

McAlary, Florence, and Judith Love Cohen. *You Can Be a Woman Marine Biologist.* Rev. ed. Marina del Rey, Calif.: Cascade Pass, Inc., 2001.

Mcghee, Karen. *National Geographic Encyclopedia of Animals.* Washington, D.C.: National Geographic Children's Books, 2006.

McKay, George. (ed.) *The Encyclopedia of Animals: A Complete Visual Guide.* Berkeley, Calif.: University of California Press, 2004.

McMillan, Beverly, and John A. Musick. *Oceans.* New York: Simon & Schuster Children's Publishing, 2007.

Needham, Bobbe. *Ecology Crafts For Kids: 50 Great Ways to Make Friends with Planet Earth.* New York: Sterling Publishing, 1998.

Peterson's. *Peterson's Summer Opportunities for Kids & Teenagers.* 26th ed. Lawrenceville, N.J.: Peterson's, 2008.

Rodd, Tony, and Jennifer Stackhouse. *Trees: A Visual Guide.* Berkeley, Calif.: University of California Press, 2008.

Rushforth, Keith, and Charles Hollis. *National Geographic Field Guide to Trees of North America.* Washington, D.C.: National Geographic Books, 2006.

Williams, Linda. *Earth Sciences Demystified.* New York: McGraw-Hill Professional, 2004.

Periodicals

Friends of the Earth Newsmagazine
http://www.foe.org

National Geographic Adventure
http://www.nationalgeographic.com/adventure

National Geographic Explorer
http://magma.nationalgeographic.com/ngexplorer

National Parks
http://www.npca.org

Nature Conservancy
http://www.nature.org/magazine

Ranger Rick
http://www.nwf.org

Sierra
http://www.sierraclub.org/sierra

Web Sites

About.com: Environmental Issues
http://environment.about.com/mbody.htm

American Camping Association: Find a Camp
http://find.acacamps.org/finding_a_camp.php

American Library Association: Great Web Sites for Kids
http://www.ala.org/greatsites

Animaland
http://www2.aspca.org/site/PageServer?pagename=kids_home

Animal Corner
http://www.animalcorner.co.uk

Animal Diversity Web
http://animaldiversity.ummz.umich.edu

Animal Fact Guide
http://www.animalfactguide.com

Backyard Nature
http://www.backyardnature.net

BBC Science & Nature
http://www.bbc.co.uk/nature

Bureau of Land Management: Adventures in the Past
http://www.blm.gov/heritage/adventures/vacation.html

Canon Envirothon
http://www.envirothon.org

CanopyMeg.com
http://www.canopymeg.com

Careers in Forestry & Natural Resources
http://www.forestrycareers.org

Dig It: The Secrets of Soil
http://forces.si.edu/soils

EcoKids
http://www.ecokids.ca

Environmental Education for Kids!
http://www.dnr.state.wi.us/eek

Environmental Protection Agency
http://www.epa.gov/epawaste/education/teens.htm

Exploratorium
http://www.exploratorium.edu

Exploring Nature Educational Resource
http://www.exploringnature.org

The Green Squad
http://www.nrdc.org/greensquad

Ground Water Adventurers
http://www.groundwateradventurers.org

Insectclopedia
http://www.insectclopedia.com

The Jane Goodall Institute
http://www.janegoodall.org

Just for Kids: Soil Biological Communities
http://www.blm.gov/nstc/soil/Kids

KidsCamps.com
http://www.kidscamps.com

Kids Go Wild
http://www.kidsgowild.com

Kids' Planet
http://www.kidsplanet.org

Magic Porthole
http://www.magicporthole.org

National Park Service: Interpretation and Education
http://www.nps.gov/learn

National Park Service: Nature and Science
http://www.nature.nps.gov

National Wildlife Federation
http://www.nwf.org/kids

The Nature Conservancy
http://www.nature.org

Oakland Zoo: Animals
http://www.oaklandzoo.org/animals

PBS: American Field Guide
http://www.pbs.org/americanfieldguide

Planting Science.org
http://www.plantingscience.org

Schoolyard Geology
http://education.usgs.gov/schoolyard

Sea Grant Marine Careers
http://www.marinecareers.net

Seaworld: Animals
http://www.seaworld.org

Sierra Club
http://www.sierraclub.org

Underground Adventure
http://www.fieldmuseum.org/undergroundadventure

World Wildlife Fund
http://www.worldwildlife.org

Yahoo!: Kids: Animals
http://kids.yahoo.com/animals

Index